THE LITTLE BROOMSTICK

Nothing *could ever happen here, thought Mary, exiled to Great-Aunt Charlotte's house. But she was wrong. That very day, Tib the cat led her to a curious flower called fly-by-night. Then she found a little broomstick hidden in a corner – her strange and wonderful magic adventure had begun.*

D1439690

Mary Stewart

The Little Broomstick

Illustrated by Shirley Hughes

KNIGHT BOOKS

the paperback division of Brockhampton Press

ISBN 0 340 17530 3

This edition published 1973 by Knight, the paperback
division of Brockhampton Press, Leicester.
Third impression 1973

Printed in Great Britain by
Richard Clay (The Chaucer Press) Ltd, Bungay, Suffolk

First published in 1971 by Brockhampton Press Ltd
Text copyright © 1971 Mary Stewart
Illustrations copyright © 1971 Brockhampton Press Ltd

This book is sold subject to the condition that it shall not by
way of trade or otherwise be lent, re-sold, hired out or otherwise
circulated without the publisher's prior consent in any form of
binding or cover other than that in which this is published and
without a similar condition including this condition being
imposed on the subsequent purchaser.

Contents

To
Troy, my resident familiar,
and Johnny, the cat who came in
from the cold

CHAPTER I
Poor Mary sat a-weeping

EVEN her name was plain. Mary Smith. Nothing could have been more depressing, she thought; to be plain, to be ten, and to be alone, staring out of her bedroom window on a grey autumn day, and to be called Mary Smith.

She was the only plain one in the family. Jenny had lovely long hair that really was the colour of gold, and everyone said Jeremy was handsome; they were older than Mary, cleverer, more attractive in every way. Moreover, they were twins, and had each other, while Mary, who was five years their junior, might as well (she thought dejectedly) have been an only child. Not that she grudged anything to them; it had always seemed to her natural that they should get things that she could not have. As now . . .

When the news had come that Daddy would have to go to America for a month towards the end of the summer holidays, and wanted Mummy to go with him, it had at first all seemed to work out beautifully. Jenny and Jeremy went off to stay with one of Jeremy's schoolfriends who had a farm in Yorkshire, and Mary was to go to Mummy's sister, Aunt Sue, who had three children aged eleven, eight, and four, and who lived within an hour's car ride of the sea.

But then, on the very day that Jenny and Jeremy had left, came the letter from Aunt Sue, saying that Uncle Gil and the two elder children were down with flu, and that consequently Aunt Sue did not feel able to risk having Mary, quite apart from all the extra work she herself was having to do . . .

So there it was. And once more the twins had got the best of it. Mary didn't grudge them the harvesting, the tractors, even the share they would have in the two elderly farm ponies; but she did think that at the very worst she might have been allowed to go and catch the flu. At least she would have been having it in company.

To Mary, sitting alone by the window on that grey autumn afternoon, flu seemed a very desirable thing indeed. She forgot about temperatures, aching bones, bed; she even forgot how tiresome Timothy, aged four, could be – and indeed was, most of the time. She only saw in her mind's eye the lovely time they would all have had together getting better, with books and games and plenty of talk and fun. She brooded over the picture, and for the fiftieth time wished to goodness she had managed to get to Aunt Sue's and catch the flu before the letter came that had sent her mother frantically to the telephone, and resulted in Mary's being bundled off – rather apologetically – to stay with Great-Aunt Charlotte in the quiet old house in the country.

Nothing, thought Mary, *nothing* could ever happen

here. If only it had been time to go to school – even school would have been better than this . . .

And she scowled out of the window at the garden where the falling leaves were rustling into a pattern on the lawn.

Great-Aunt Charlotte, who was old, kind, and very deaf, lived in a rambling red-brick house deep in Shropshire, where a mile or so of woods and cherry-orchards stretched between the garden and the main road. The orchards had once belonged to the house, but now were worked by a local firm of market gardeners, who kept the gates locked, and one wasn't supposed to go into the orchards at all. Half of the house had been let, too; the people who lived there were away on holiday, and somehow it made the place seem even lonelier and more isolated to see the shutters up, and the door – the old side-door of the Manor – blankly shut and fastened all day. The village of Redmanor, with its handful of houses clustered round the church and the post-office, was a full mile away. You got there by a narrow road that was little more than a country lane; Mary had some-times walked that way, and had never met anyone on the road yet.

In the Manor itself, Great-Aunt Charlotte lived alone, save for an elderly friend and companion, Miss Marjori-banks (pronounced Marshbanks), an elderly Scottish housekeeper called Mrs McLeod (pronounced Macloud), and an elderly Pekingese called K'ung Fû-tsze (pronounced Confucius). To be sure, there was Mrs Banks and her daughter Nancy, who came in to clean, and there was Zebedee, the old man who did the garden, but all the same, it was not a very exciting prospect for Miss Mary Smith, aged ten, and rather shy.

Miss Mary Smith was critically examining her tongue in the bedroom mirror.

It looked very healthy. And she felt fine.

She put it in, sighed, then put it out again at her reflection, and went downstairs to find something to do.

Miss Marjoribanks was in the drawing-room, sorting embroidery silks on the wide window seat. There was a rather poor fire in the grate, and in front of this sat Confucius, sulking a little and digesting his lunch. Great-Aunt Charlotte was sitting in her wing chair to one side of the fire, presumably also digesting her lunch, but looking a great deal more pleasant about it than Confucius. She was asleep.

Mary tiptoed across to the window seat.

She sat down quietly.

She watched Miss Marjoribanks disentangle a length of puce silk from a skein of soft rust-red. The colours were horrible together. Miss Marjoribanks twisted and shook and tugged, and finally cheated by cutting both silks with the embroidery scissors. She began to wind them on little twists of newspaper.

Mary opened her mouth to whisper an offer of help.

Immediately Miss Marjoribanks fixed her with a faded pale blue eye. 'Sssh!' she hissed. 'You'll wake Confucius!' She moved the box of silks a little further away from Mary. 'And Confucius,' she added as an afterthought, 'will wake your great-aunt.'

'But —' began Mary.

'Sssh!' said Miss Marjoribanks.

Mary tiptoed out of the drawing-room, and took at

least two and a half minutes to close the door without a sound.

She found Mrs McLeod in the kitchen, making an upside-down cake. She was standing at the big scrubbed table, beating something in a yellow bowl. She hardly seemed to notice Mary's shy entry; she was talking to herself, apparently in a foreign language. Or it could – thought Mary suddenly, looking from Mrs McLeod's gaunt face and skinny arms to the pan that simmered on the stove – it could be a spell.

'Twa oz floor,' muttered Mrs McLeod, beating vigorously, 'an' B.P., a wee puckle o' salt, shoogar – aye, that's a'.'

'What are you making?' asked Mary.

Mrs McLeod jumped, so that the wooden spoon clattered against the basin, and on the table the tins of salt and baking powder and sugar rattled.

'Maircy me!' she exclaimed. 'Ye fair startled me, lassie! I niver haird ye come in! What wad ye be wanting noo?'

She resumed her beating of the mixture, and her eye went back to the page of a battered recipe book which was in front of her, propped against a bowl of eggs.

'Time was,' she said, 'when I could mind the lot without looking. But no' ony mair. Twa oz melted bu'er —'

'I wondered if I could help?' said Mary, edging a little nearer. 'I sometimes help Mummy bake at home, you know. She gives me a bit of pastry and I —'

'Nay, then,' said the housekeeper, but not unkindly. 'I'm no' making paste the day. Only this for the denner, and it's a verra compulcated thing at that. Can ye no' rin oot and play in the gairden? It's no' cauld for all it's grey.'

She ran a floury finger down the page of the book, and frowned at the recipe again.

'Bu'er,' she said. 'And yin an' a half eggs well beaten. *Half* an egg . . . Did ye ever hear the like o' that?'

'The white half or the yellow half?' asked Mary, peering at the book.

But at this moment something spat and sizzled on the stove, and the housekeeper, dropping her spoon, darted across the kitchen and grabbed a pan from the burner.

'I'll be burnin' the apricots next,' she said. 'Now rin awa, lassie, and play in the gairden; if you talk to me here I'll spoil the cake! I canna dae twa things at yince.'

Mary went slowly out, through the scullery, to the back door.

Mrs Banks's daughter Nancy was taking down washing off the line. She was a big plump girl with round red arms and bright brown eyes. She smiled at Mary over an armful of pillow-cases, and greeted her in her soft Shropshire voice.

'Can I help hang the clothes out?' asked Mary, picking up two fallen clothes-pegs and dropping them with the others in the pocket of Nancy's apron.

Nancy laughed. 'They be dry mostly,' she said in her lilting voice. 'Mother and I be ironing now.'

She pulled the prop from under the line, and it swung down within reach. She unpegged the last two sheets, and dropped the pegs into her pocket, just as her mother's voice, lifted shrilly, came from the wash-house.

'Nancy! Fetch them sheets now, do!'

'I'm coming, Ma!' called Nancy, and with another smile at Mary she vanished through the wash-house door.

If Mary had not been searching for Zebedee, the gardener, it is probable that she would never have seen him, for, like all good gardeners, he seemed to be not a person, but merely a part of the landscape. In his faded jacket and battered old hat, with string knotted round the knees of his trousers, he looked like something that had been left lying about in the potting-shed; under the shadow of the awful old hat his cheekbones were plant-pot-red, and the backs of his gnarled old hands, where the veins and bones were all a-tangle, could have been twisted out of the same yellow raffia he used to tie up the chrysanthemums.

Which is what he was doing when at last Mary found him.

A shaft of autumn sunshine had parted the grey overcast sky, and was gilding the trees and the fallen leaves that rustled as she walked across the lawn. In front of a tall hedge of cypress the chrysanthemums nodded heads of bronze and copper and sulphur-yellow, while from them and from the earth and dead leaves and the tangle of bright nasturtiums round their roots, came the sad, beautiful smell of autumn.

Zebedee, pausing for a moment in his work, peered at her through the flowers with bright old eyes, like a robin, but he said nothing. The tousled heads of the chrysanthemums nodded as he pulled the raffia round the stems and knotted it. He bent down again and vanished behind the flowers. Mary stood at the edge of the lawn, and spoke hesitatingly.

'Can I help tie them up too?'

The chrysanthemums shook again, and a ball of raffia flew out towards her.

She picked it up, and took a doubtful step forward. Zebedee's awful old hat reappeared suddenly three clumps farther down the border, behind an enormous scarlet dahlia; his back was towards her, and his hands rustled busily down among the leaves.

Mary glanced again at the ball of raffia, decided that it must be an invitation to help, and, pushing aside the Michaelmas daisies and the big, flaring dahlias, made her way to the back of the border among the chrysanthemums.

She began slowly, carefully, to knot the raffia to the stakes, and then to thread it round the stems of the plants so that the leaves would not be crushed. Old Zebedee had vanished again, but – as if it were his familiar spirit – a robin flew out of the cypress hedge and perched on a dahlia-stake, watching her with the same old bright eyes.

The shaft of sunlight moved slowly through the coloured tangle of flowers and fading leaves. The Virginia creeper on the walls of the Manor glinted richly like silk tapestry, and the tall chimneys, catching the late sun, glowed warmly against the pewter-dark sky behind them.

Then Mary, pulling the raffia too tightly, broke the stem of a chrysanthemum.

It was a tall plant, perhaps the tallest and finest of all, and it went with a snap that almost echoed in the still air. The huge amber-gold mop of blossom hung dismally, dragging on the earth and rotting leaves.

Mary stared in dismay.

And suddenly, as suddenly as he had vanished, old

Zebedee appeared at her elbow, surveying the wreck of his prize with disgust and anger.

'I ought'a known better,' he said bitterly, and his voice, like the rest of him, was part of the garden. It was thin and wheezy but queerly musical, like the wind in the eaves. 'I ought'a known better. Childer and dogs be no manner of use to a garden. You best let be.'

'I'm sorry,' said Mary dolefully, and, handing him back his raffia-ball, she turned disconsolately away.

She found a gap in the cypress hedge, and a wicket-gate giving on a path that wound away from the garden into the surrounding woods.

This she followed, aimlessly, with her loneliness pressing harder and harder upon her as she went on through the greenish shadow, her feet noiseless upon the damp carpet of brown and yellow leaves. To one side a young oak thrust a fist-full of acorns over the path, with the last pale leaves fluttering round them, ready to fall. In a cup made by the crotch of a beech-root stood a pool of black water, where a thistle-puff floated. Above this, like a roof, jutted the orange fans of some big fungus, and pallid toadstools crowded together in damp bunches among the moss and mud and rotting twigs.

Everywhere was damp, and decay, and the end of summer.

Mary stopped, and the silence of the dying woods hung heavily round her. An acorn, falling from its cup on to the mosses, made, in that stillness, a tap loud enough to make you jump.

Then suddenly, neat and quiet and graceful as a dancer, there strolled into the middle of the path a small black cat.

He was completely black from ears to tail-tip; his toes were black, and his whiskers, and the aristocratic eyebrow-hairs that stood above his green, green eyes.

He stood in the very middle of the path, and he looked at Mary. Then his mouth opened to show a triangle of pink tongue and very white teeth, and he made a remark.

Probably a very ordinary remark, thought Mary, like 'How do you do?' or 'Nice day, isn't it?' But the cat obviously expected an answer, so she said: 'How do you do? My name's Mary Smith. What's yours?'

The cat made no reply. There were more important things, obviously, to do. He turned his back on Mary, with his tail held politely in the air, and walked away down the path, deeper into the wood. But he walked, not as if he were leaving her, but as if he wanted her to follow him.

Mary, delighted to have found a companion where she least expected, followed, but without attempting to touch the cat. He obviously knew exactly where he was going, and just as obviously he had something important to do, so to stroke him as you might have stroked an ordinary cat would have seemed insulting.

And presently the cat turned aside from the path, slipped under a hanging huddle of snowberries, and leaped on to a fallen branch of oak. He balanced there, looking back at Mary as with some difficulty she pushed past the snowberry bush.

She approached the oak branch. The cat did not move, but watched her closely.

Then she gave an exclamation of surprise and pleasure. For there in the hidden corner behind the snowberries, growing in the shelter of the fallen bough, was a little clump of flowers such as she had never seen before.

The leaves, set in stiff rosettes, were of a curious bluish-green, mottled like frogs, and above them on slender stems hung the flowers, clusters of graceful purple bells, whose throats were streaked with silver, and whose pistils, like long tongues, thrust out of the freaked throats in stabs of bright gold.

Mary knelt down on the fallen branch and gazed at the flowers, while beside her sat the little black cat waving his black tail, and watching her out of his green, green eyes.

CHAPTER II

Things that go bump in the night

THE little cat, dignified as ever, was still with Mary when at length she came back to the house, bearing in one hand a single stem of the strange purple flower that she had found in the wood.

She went through the back way. The wash-house door was shut, which meant presumably that Mrs Banks and Nancy had gone back to their home in the village. But old Zebedee was in the scullery, sitting on a box, with an ancient, crusted-looking pail gripped between his knees. This was full of some thick steaming mess, at which he pounded fiercely with a stick. He still had on his awful old hat.

He peered at her now from under the brim. Mary, remembering the broken chrysanthemum, approached him a little nervously, holding out the purple flower.

'Do you know what this is, please?' she asked, hesitating. 'I found it in the wood. I've never seen anything like it before.'

Zebedee's bright eyes regarded her. He did not seem to be bearing any malice about the broken plant. He chuckled.

'Aye. It do grow in the wood, surely. Though I've not laid eye to it for many a year. Where did you get it?'

'Not far from the path. Actually, the cat found it.'

'The cat?' repeated Zebedee. 'Oh, aye.'

The little black cat looked at him, aloofly, and began to wash a whisker.

'What's he called?' asked Mary.

'The cat? Or the flower?'

'The – well, both, actually.'

Old Zebedee began to stir the contents of the bucket again.

'He don't come to the house much, the cat,' he said. 'He don't rightly belong here; he just came in one day, out of the wood. I calls him Tib.'

'Tib,' said Mary, experimenting.

The cat stopped washing for a moment, flicked her a glance, and then went on massaging his ear.

'Two on 'em, there was,' said Zebedee. 'Black 'un and grey, but the same size, same eyes, and like as two peas. Tib and Gib, I called them.'

'I haven't seen a grey one.'

'Likely he's settled in the village.' Zebedee nodded. ''Tis a way cats have, pick a good home and settle there, and nothing can shift 'em. I seen the pair of 'em last week, side by side on the Vicarage wall in the dark, like a couple o' gilli-howlets.'

'A couple of what?'

'Church owls, you'd call 'em. Barn owls. I reckon they be twins. Tib and Gib, I calls 'em.'

Mary glanced at Tib. He had stopped washing and was sitting perfectly still, watching her. His eyes looked greener than ever.

'I do hope he stays here!' she said. 'Tib, you will stay with me, won't you? They don't *belong* to the Vicarage, do they, Zebedee? Perhaps if I went and asked —'

'Cats doesn't belong,' said Zebedee. 'They goes where they wants to. Gib-cat's keeping the Vicar's kitchen warm, I reckon, but this little black 'un – been haunting the garden here regular now for days. Mebbe he'll settle here now he's got company.'

'But what about Confucius? Miss Marshbanks says he doesn't like cats.'

Zebedee gave that wheezy laugh that seemed to whistle through his lungs like wind through far-away trees. 'Never a dog yet that could so much as stare out a cat,' he said. 'And that Tib-cat could stare out a King, I reckon.'

'Well, if he'll stay, he and I can go and look for Gib tomorrow,' said Mary. 'It'll be something to – I'll enjoy doing that. And he seems pretty good at finding things. Did you say you knew the name of the flower?'

Zebedee dug in the bucket with his stick. He chuckled again.

'First time as ye goes into the wood,' he said, 'and ye finds it. I mind my Dad telling me how folks used to come far and wide to gather it in Redmanor woods; years back, that'd be, when chemists and doctors and such wasn't to be found on every bush, and country folks made their own simples.' He peered, nodding at the stem of blossom. 'Aye, that's her, a rare one, surely, and sought for high and low. 'Tis the only place she grows, they say, and she only flowers once in seven years.'

Mary stared at him.

'Only once in seven years?'

'Aye. A rare one, surely.'

'What did the – the folk use it for?' asked Mary.

Old Zebedee shook his head and stirred the pail again. 'Potions and powders – that I couldn't say. But the word went that there was magic in her.'

'Magic?'

'It be but a tale, a country tale,' said Zebedee. 'The flower, she be in the books, likely enough, with a grand name as long as your arm, and foreign at that. But with her flowering at the seventh year, and at the time when the other flowers is dying – well, superstitious folks called her magic. And 'tis said that in the olden days the witches sought her from the corners of the Black Mountains, and from the place where the old city was and there's now naught but a pool o' water.'

The words fell queerly in the clean, everyday scullery, with bright packets of soap powder on a shelf, and a rack of aluminium pans above them, and with the late pale shaft of the sun falling across the scrubbed floor.

Mary stared down at the flowers clustered on the slender stem, and in the small draught from the door the purple heads stirred, and the golden tongues moved in the silver throats.

'A magic flower . . .' She touched a pistil gently with a forefinger. 'Look, Zebedee, the gold comes off . . . What's the flower's name?'

'I told you,' said the old man. 'I don't know the name in the books, and folks don't hunt her now the way they used to, but when I was a lad she had names a-plenty – dragon-tongue, witch's bells, tibsroot —'

'Tibsroot!' cried Mary. 'That's the cat! Tib! He found it for me!'

Zebedee chuckled again. 'Likely he's a witch's cat,' he said indulgently. 'He do look like one, surely. That be why I called him Tib. Likely his name's only Blackie or Smuts or Sooty, after all.'

'He *looks* like a Tib,' said Mary stoutly. 'And I'm sure he's a magic cat. Look how he found the magic flower for me – the tibsroot.'

'That's one name for it,' said Zebedee. 'I calls it fly-by-night.'

'Why?'

But he would not answer, and when she questioned him, he only stirred his bucket so violently that at last she said, 'What's in the bucket, Zebedee?'

'Pollard for the hens,' he said shortly. 'Nasty critters. Nasty mean pecking critters, hens. I hates hens.'

And, picking up his bucket, he stumped out of the scullery.

Mary watched him go, then turned to look for Tib. But the scullery was empty, and when she ran to the back door to peer out into the yard, that was empty, too.

The little black cat had vanished.

It was late that night, when Mary had been in bed for some time, and when she should certainly have been asleep, that the queer thing happened.

She had woken, drowsy and warm from her first sleep, and was just turning over towards the window, when she heard it.

Distant, over the trees. A swish like the swoop of wind.

'That's funny,' thought Mary. 'There isn't any wind. There must be a storm coming. What a pity, when I was going with Tib tomorrow —'

The noise came again, louder, nearer.

A long shrill rush of wind, with a whistle in it, and all along the wall of the house the Virginia creeper swished as if giant fingers had swept along it, and the windows rattled.

Mary stiffened, her skin tingling.

Then, suddenly, the scream.

A thud, and the scream checked as if the screamer had bitten through his tongue.

Silence.

And as Mary, with every inch of her flesh crawling with goose-pimples, sat slowly up in bed, staring at the window, there came a faint scrabbling noise on the sill.

Rigid with fright, she sat motionless, then slowly, slowly reached out a hand to the switch of the bedside light.

She found it, took a deep breath, and pressed it. The room sprang into light, and the black sky outside the window drew back. But something, black as the night sky, moved upon the window-sill. Something tapped and scrabbled at the window. Two eyes glared . . .

Mary's breath went out in a great sigh of relief as she flung herself out of bed and towards the window.

'Tib! Tib! Oh, Tib, what a fright you gave me!'

She threw open the bottom of the window, and the little black cat leaped into the room. Ignoring Mary, he stalked into the middle of the carpet and stood there, his tail lashing, his fur stiff with fury, his eyes as bright as traffic-lights.

Mary bent over him.

'Tib, what's the matter? What's happened?'

Tib took no notice of her. His fur still bristled like a

hearth-brush; the green eyes still glared at the window. Mary switched off the light, then went back to the window and stared out into the dark garden.

The trees were a dim shadowed huddle beyond the lawn. The hanging clouds above them had withdrawn a little, to show, beyond, a faint inlay of silver star-dust. The air was motionless. Two storeys below, on the darkness of the lawn, nothing stirred.

It had only been a gust of wind, after all.

And the thud, the scream? Mary closed the window and, picking up Tib, began to smooth his angry fur. A cat-fight, probably. They did scream, terribly, when they fought. Perhaps Gib had come back, and they had had a quarrel. Even twins quarrelled sometimes. Jenny and Jeremy certainly did.

'We'll find him tomorrow, and then you'll have to make it up,' she told Tib.

She climbed into bed then, and Tib, purring suddenly, curled warm and soft against her.

Just as the two of them were settling down to sleep together, Mary thought of something. 'Tib,' she said, whispering in the dark against the velvet fur, 'Tib. *How did you get up there on my window-sill?*'

Tib, settling a purring nose among his curled black paws, did not reply.

CHAPTER III
One misty, moisty morning

THE morning, again, was grey. The clouds, which during the night had sifted so beautifully away from the stars, had closed again, and the dahlias hung heavy scarlet heads in the still air.

Mary could see them from the breakfast-room window, deep red against the cypress hedge. Tib, who had come downstairs with her, was not interested in the dahlias. He had demanded – and received – a saucer of milk, which Mary rather guiltily hoped he would finish before Miss Marjoribanks came down to breakfast. Great-Aunt Charlotte, who never fussed about anything, always breakfasted in her bedroom.

'Hurry, Tib, please,' whispered Mary.

But Tib was enjoying his breakfast, and was not going to hurry for anyone. His small pink tongue took up the milk in the daintiest, tiniest laps imaginable, all from the very edge of the saucer. And at least a quarter of every lap – Mary noticed with dismay – was going over on to the floor.

Miss Marjoribanks' voice sounded briskly from the doorway.

'Good morning, my dear. Have you had your breakfast?'

Mary jumped and turned. Tib took no notice, except to lap a little more milk on to the floor.

'Good morning, Miss Marjoribanks. No, not yet.'

'Marshbanks,' said that lady crisply. 'Well, come along, sit down. We'll have it together.' Apparently she hadn't noticed Tib and his saucer. She moved briskly towards the head of the table. All her movements as a rule were as brisk and decided as her speech, but Mary noticed, as she followed her to the table, that there was a certain air of carefulness this morning in the way Miss Marjoribanks walked which indicated an unusual stiffness of the joints. Indeed, Miss Marjoribanks sat down with what could only be called the most extreme caution. Then she poured out tea, and they began breakfast.

Great-Aunt Charlotte's companion was the very opposite of her friend and employer, both in manner and appearance. She was rather small and thin, but she was alert, decisive, talkative and – it must be admitted – rather managing. She managed the housekeeper, the Bankses, and the tradespeople. She managed Great-Aunt Charlotte, who was fat and placid and easy-going. She even managed the Vicar of Redmanor, though it could not truthfully be said that she managed the Vicar's wife. She did not manage old Zebedee, the gardener, because she never met him; when he saw her coming he faded, like a zebra or a deer or a stick insect, into the landscape. And Mary suspected that she would find it difficult to manage Tib, the witch's cat.

Tib, who had finished his milk now, drew Miss Marjoribanks' attention to it by thanking Mary politely, and then jumping on to the window seat where, with the utmost self-possession, he began to wash his face.

And Miss Marjoribanks, far from looking cross, was eyeing him uneasily – almost (thought Mary) nervously.

'That cat,' she said sharply, 'does not belong to the house. How did it get in?'

Tib looked at Mary. Mary decided to respect his confidence.

'I had him in my room,' she said truthfully. 'He must have come into the house in the night.'

Miss Marjoribanks looked at Tib again, and Tib resumed his washing in an odiously detached manner. The expression on his face could only be described as a smirk. Miss Marjoribanks looked away, and moved uneasily in her chair.

'I'm sure,' she said, 'that your Great-Aunt Charlotte would not like it, dear, your having a cat in your bedroom. But perhaps' – she paused over her scrambled egg and turned her sharp, pale-blue gaze on Mary – 'perhaps you are a little lonely here, with just a lot of old people?'

Mary began, politely, to protest, but Miss Marjoribanks cut her short.

'Of course you are! And it's quite understandable, my dear, quite understandable; this is not a house for children. Not for a child on her own, that is – though for a *family* of you there would no doubt be plenty to do . . . places to explore, and so on.' She nodded kindly at Mary. 'Such a pity the Vicar is away on holiday now. It would have been splendid for you to have a playmate . . . such a beautiful garden, too, and goes right down to the river.'

It seemed a little odd to Mary (remembering the

nice, silver-haired old clergyman who had taken matins last Sunday) that even Miss Marjoribanks should consider him a suitable playmate for a ten-year-old, but Miss Marjoribanks obviously knew very little about children, and was just as obviously trying to be kind, so Mary said nothing. Then suddenly she remembered what Zebedee had told her about the two cats on the Vicarage wall. Perhaps Tib and Gib belonged there, and had come wandering over here to find food? Perhaps Gib was still out in the woods, alone and hungry? She glanced at Tib, to see that he had stopped washing, and was watching her attentively, as if he could follow her thoughts.

'Is the Vicarage empty, then?' she asked.

'Oh, no,' said Miss Marjoribanks. 'No, indeed. Old Mr Spenser – whom you saw on Sunday – is living there while the Vicar and his family are away. The poor Vicar can't just go away for a holiday and leave his parish, you know. He has to find someone to take the services for him.'

'Oh, I see.' Mary fastened on the one thing that mattered. 'There are children, then?'

'One – a son, Peter. About your age, I think. *Such* a pity,' said Miss Marjoribanks again, 'that they're away.'

'When will they be back?'

'That I cannot say, my dear. But perhaps I can find out today. Which brings me to what I had to tell you.' She set down her cup and began to roll up her table napkin. 'Today your great-aunt and I have promised to go and see an old, old friend. An *old, old* friend,' she added, to make this quite clear. 'And it is a long-standing engagement, so I am afraid that you will be left quite alone today.'

'I shall be all right,' said Mary. 'I'll play with Tib, and help in the garden, and – and things.'

The companion patted her hand. 'Tomorrow we will think out something for you. We will go somewhere . . . something . . . a picnic, perhaps?' Her eye lingered doubtfully on the grey autumn sky.

But Mary caught at the suggestion with pleasure.

'Could I? Could I do that today, Miss Marjori – Marshbanks, please? I could go into the woods, and it would be lovely if I had my lunch with me. And even if there's no sun today, it's very warm! Could I, please?'

Miss Marjoribanks considered for a moment.

'I don't see why not,' she said at length. 'Though September – but so warm, even stuffy – yes, of course you may, dear child. I shall speak to Mrs McLeod and she will give you some sandwiches. As long as you don't go too far and get lost —'

'I shan't do that,' said Mary. 'But I've been wanting to explore the woods.' She suddenly remembered the purple 'fly-by-night', which was standing in a tooth-glass in her bedroom. Perhaps Miss Marjoribanks knew its real name. 'I found —' she began, but at this moment Great-Aunt Charlotte came in, and the sentence stayed in mid-air.

'Dear child,' said Great-Aunt Charlotte comfortably, kissing her. 'How are you this morning?'

Mary admitted that she was much the same as yesterday.

'And did you sleep well?' asked Great-Aunt Charlotte, in the calm, flat voice of the very deaf.

'Very well, thank you, Aunt Charlotte. I woke up once —'

'What woke you?' asked Miss Marjoribanks sharply. Mary was startled at her tone.

'Oh, a noise – a cat-fight, I think,' she said, and Miss Marjoribanks sat back, apparently satisfied. 'And an awful thump,' added Mary.

'A lump?' said Great-Aunt Charlotte. 'In your bed? Oh dear, that will never do. I wonder if another mattress —'

'Not a lump, Aunt Charlotte, a *thump*!' said Mary loudly.

'Yes dear, I know. Such a pity. There's nothing more annoying than a lumpy bed,' said Great-Aunt Charlotte.

At this moment further explanations were prevented by the entry into the breakfast-room, wheezing and waddling, of Great-Aunt Charlotte's elderly and – we might as well admit it – rather unpleasant dog, Confucius.

And – at one and the same moment – Confucius saw Tib, and Tib saw Confucius.

'Oh dear!' said Great-Aunt Charlotte, making an ineffectual grab for Confucius.

'Oh dear me!' cried Miss Marjoribanks, starting to rise briskly from her chair, then, with a wince, rising rather slowly.

'Oh!' cried Mary, who did not care at all for Confucius, but a good deal for Tib.

But nobody need have worried. Tib, the witch's cat, merely gave the Pekingese what will have to be described as A Look, and Confucius, who had darted forward, slobbering with pleasure and excitement, stopped short, remembered that he had a pressing engagement somewhere quite different, and went out with what was supposed to be careless dignity, but looked like a hasty shuffle.

Tib smirked, tidied away a whisker, and suggested to Mary that she should open the window to let him take his morning stroll across the lawn.

So it came about that soon after Great-Aunt Charlotte and her companion had driven away to visit the old, old friend, Mary, with sandwiches in her coat pocket, went out into the garden to look for Tib and Zebedee.

Tib was nowhere to be seen, but she found Zebedee straight away. He was wheeling a barrow along between the lawn and the side of the house.

'Good morning,' said Mary. 'Please, have you seen Tib anywhere?'

Zebedee shook his head and went on trundling. Mary trotted along beside the barrow.

'We were going to look for Gib today, you see,' she explained, 'only Tib went out after breakfast, and I can't find him anywhere.'

'Happen he'll turn up,' said Zebedee, still trundling. 'Cats do.'

'Can I help you again, then, please?'

'And break me flowers, likely?' said Zebedee, but he gave her a not unpleasant look from beneath the brim of the awful hat.

'No, truly. Isn't there something easy I can do?'

Zebedee set down the barrow, and took out of it a spade, a fork, and a garden-broom made of twigs tied to a stout handle.

'There be leaves to sweep,' he said, and handed her the broom. 'A bad untidy month this be, September.

There. Happen you can't do much harm sweeping – if you don't break my broomstick forbye.'

He gave the little wheeze that passed for a chuckle, and taking the spade, he began to dig the border under the windows of the house.

Mary began to sweep up the leaves.

It sounded such a simple job, but soon she discovered, as she struggled with the enormous besom, that it was not only difficult, but nearly impossible. She began by trying to sweep round her in great half-circles, but the leaves merely curled under the broom-twigs, and rustled happily back into their drifts under the trees. Then she seized the broomstick – which was some inches taller than she was – just above the head of twigs, and tried sweeping in short upright strokes, but this was exhausting, and merely seemed to have the effect of scattering the leaves further afield.

And when she had at last scraped together a respect-able pile of leaves, Tib, suddenly reappearing from somewhere, flung himself into the middle of it, rolled over twice, threw two pawfuls of dead leaves into the air, turned round three times, and darted off sideways with his tail held up like a question-mark.

'Oh, Tib!' cried Mary, in exasperation. 'And you needn't think I'm coming to play with you now, after that! You can just wait till I've finished this job!'

So she laboured on, and at length managed to get a good pile of leaves into the barrow, which she trundled off the way Tib had gone, towards the compost heap by the wall of the kitchen garden.

She could not manage to tip the barrow, but she scooped her load out somehow and then was about to take up the shafts for the return journey, when her eye was caught by something flung carelessly among the sticks and rubbish of a waiting bonfire further along the wall.

It was a little broomstick.

Mary ran to the bonfire and pulled the little broom off the pile. It was just a perfect size for her, light and weildy, with a head of good stiff birch-twigs. Pleased, she flung it on the barrow, and wheeled her find back to the lawn.

'Zebedee, look what I've found!' she called, but the old gardener was once again invisible.

And so was Tib. At least Mary thought so, until a crackling and swaying high up in a lime tree showed her the small black cat balancing delicately along a high bough.

'Do be careful, Tib!' she cried, but soon, seeing how easily and lightly he moved, she went back to her task, and the leaves piled up in obedient drifts under the strokes of the little broomstick.

The day, though grey, was sultry, and over the heavy-hanging leaves of the trees the sky brooded low, in great sagging spans of cloud. Now and again, rustling in the still air, leaves of lime and oak and copper beech would release their hold, and come floating down to swell the drifts of rust and ochre on the lawn. Somewhere, shrilly, the robin began to sing.

One more barrow-load, thought Mary, then she would call Tib down from the lime tree, and they would go off together into the woods for lunch. Zebedee had already gone for his; there was no sign of him.

She paused in her work and stood for a moment, leaning on the broomstick. The day was certainly warm. She pushed the hair back out of her eyes, and, as she did so, noticed a gleam of purple in the grass. A single fly-by-night flower was lying there. It must have fallen yesterday as she carried her prize home.

She picked it up.

But the flower, grown soft, crushed in her hand, and on her fingers the juice from its petals ran purple and red, and gold-dusty from the yellow tongue. She dropped the squashed flower into her pocket, and rubbed her sticky hand sharply down the handle of the broom.

And turned back to her sweeping.

Then it happened.

At the touch of the purple juice the little broomstick gave a leap, a violent twist, a kick like the kick of a pony. Instinctively Mary clung to it, but it had twisted between her legs, and she fell.

But she never reached the ground.

For as she tipped forward, clinging along the handle of the little besom, with the head of twigs between her knees, the broomstick reared, shook itself violently, and then soared up towards the treetops with a swish like the rustle of a little wind.

And as it tore past the upper boughs, with Mary clinging for dear life to the handle, there was a scream and a crackle of twigs, and, with paws stretched like a flying squirrel, Tib flung himself out of the lime tree and on to the back of the besom. The broomstick jerked slightly under the impact, and then tore on, up, straight as a spear, towards the sagging clouds.

CHAPTER IV

Up above the world so high

THEN all at once they had reached the cloud, had
burst through its low edges, and were tearing through
the swirling grey. What had seemed to be a canopy of
cloud sagging like wet canvas proved, as the flying
broomstick speared into it, to be a whirling, tossing mass
of lighted foam. The broomstick rode it like a sea,
ripping soundlessly through the foggy eddies, while the
mist streamed out behind like spindrift in a speedboat's
wake.

'Oh, Tib!' screamed Mary, and her words were
whirled away to drown in the rushing cloud. 'Tib, what
shall we do? It's a *witch's broom*!'

There was no answer from Tib, and Mary, alarmed
in case he had fallen in their mad flight upwards,
twisted her head to look. This made the broomstick rock
so violently that, terrified, she gave up the attempt, and
concentrated all her attention on gripping the shaft of
the broom with hands and knees.

But out of the corner of her eye she had caught a glimpse of Tib, flattened along the broom-twigs like a black slug, his claws driven deep into the wood, his green eyes blazing, and his black tail streaming behind like a pennant.

Then suddenly, with a rush like a lift, they hurtled up out of the misty grey into the blazing sunshine. The broomstick, slackening speed, levelled off and began to cruise smoothly along over the upper surface of the cloud.

Above them arched the immense and brilliant sky, and around, on every hand as far as the eye could reach, stretched a dazzle of cloud like a floor of living snow and tossing rainbow spray.

Mary gasped with wonder, fear, and excitement, as her strange steed sailed easily across the sparkling floor of the sky.

'And I said nothing could happen! But Tib, how on earth do we get *down*?'

As if in reply, the broomstick veered slightly to the left, and Mary heard Tib spit with annoyance as a clawhold slipped.

Straight ahead towered a cumulus cloud, a thunder-head. It seemed to be bearing down upon them, slowly, like a majestic and enormous iceberg thrusting through piling floes. But between the white sea over which they sailed, and the flashing base of the thunderhead, Mary could glimpse a gulf, a great dark-green gap in the cloud, like a chasm. Towards this, with a quiver that shook it from tip to bristles, the magic broomstick headed at an increasing rate.

'Tib!' shrieked Mary. 'Hang on! I think we're going down – Oh!'

This last exclamation as the broomstick, with a sudden rush, flew straight out from the edge of cloud, over the green gulf that fell away below.

Mary caught a glimpse, framed in a ring of cloud, of green country, silver-threaded with rivers, stretched like a map away beneath . . . then the whole expanse veered, tilted, and swung up as the broomstick dropped its nose and went into a long dive.

Down, down, down . . . and the air tore the breath out of her body as she tried to crouch closer to the broomstick.

Down, down, down, and the green-and-silver map came rushing up to meet her . . . became green hills and curving rivers . . . became woods and fields and hedge-rows . . . became copses and trees and banks of flowers . . . till presently she was sailing past the leafy treetops, and the broomstick, levelling out once more, ran at a rapidly dwindling speed above the hedges of a curling lane.

The hedge on the left gave way to a high wall with a gate in it, a huge gate flanked by pillars where stone griffins ramped. The gate was shut, but the little broomstick sailed easily over it, missed a griffin's upraised paw by about six inches, then cruised across the wooded park towards a distant glimpse of chimneys at the end of the long driveway.

Soon Mary could see the house clearly. It was a biggish building which looked as if it had once been a castle. It was built of grey stone, and had battlements, but in places it had been mended with red brick, and the top of the biggest tower had been taken off and replaced with a glass dome shaped like an onion, while yet another tower had a flat roof with something jutting from it that looked uncommonly like a diving-board.

In the centre of the main block of the building was a wide flight of steps leading up to a big door. To one side of this centre block stretched a lower wing of buildings; these were one storey high and looked modern. On the other side, the right as they approached, was what looked like the old stableyard; this was a cobbled court-yard green with weeds, surrounded by stables and coach-house and approached from the park by an arched tunnel crowned with a clock-tower where a gilded weathercock spun in an agitated manner.

As if, thought Mary, the little broomstick were a magnet, and its approach set a compass-needle spin-ning . . .

The broomstick banked to avoid the clock-tower, skimmed the coach-house roof, then sank smoothly down to a perfect landing.

Somewhere, excitedly, a cock was crowing.

Mary's feet went thankfully out to either side to touch the solid earth.

'Oh, Tib —!' she began again, but never finished the sentence, because the little broomstick proceeded, quite methodically, to buck her off.

At the first buck Tib sprang, with a startled hiss, to the ground. At the second Mary, flying through the air, landed with a thump on the weedy cobbles, right at the feet of a little man who, from his seat on an ancient mounting-block, had watched the whole proceeding with a complete lack of surprise.

CHAPTER V
Ride a cock-horse

HE was a strange little man, not a dwarf, but made on so small a scale, so thin and wizened and bent in on himself, that he was scarcely as big as Mary. He had a sharp, brown face, lined and seamed like cracked leather, and his eyes were small and green and shining. He was dressed in wrinkled breeches and an old green jacket.

As Mary, feeling shaken, puzzled, and remarkably foolish, picked herself up from the cobbles, the little man took a straw from his mouth, and spoke.

'You'll be needing a few lessons,' he said.

Mary dusting down her coat, stared at him.

'Lessons?'

He nodded. 'Riding lessons. You shouldn't have tumbled off like that – though it's not a good ride, that besom. Tricky. You were lucky to get as far as this.'

Here he addressed the broomstick sharply, in what sounded like a foreign language. It had been frisking about nearby, but when the little man spoke it dropped to the ground and lay still.

He got off the mounting-block and picked it up.

'But I don't understand!' cried Mary. 'Who are you? Where *is* this? How did it happen?'

The little man paid no attention. He patted the broomstick, and tucked it under one arm. 'It'll stand quiet now, but we'd better be putting it in the stable till you'll be wanting it again. Come and I'll show you.'

And, carrying the broomstick, he led the way across the yard to where a half-door stood shut and bolted across the dark interior of a stable. He undid the half-door and led the way in. Mary followed. In the shaft of sunlight that sloped through the open door, motes of dust danced like fireflies. The floor was of ribbed stone, and there was a pleasing muddle of boxes and straw and sacks and ropes, such as you might find in any stable. There were even empty hay-racks fixed to the wall. But no horses.

Against the wall opposite the door, each in a little compartment like a bicycle-stand, stood about a dozen brooms. Some were battered, and old-fashioned in design like Mary's, while some looked almost new.

Towards these the little man, as he propped Mary's broomstick between two big, rather grubby garden besoms, gestured with contempt.

'Modern stuff,' he said, with a twist of his leathery face. 'Mechanised, that's the word they use for it. Goes much faster, of course, but give me a good old-fashioned besom that takes a bit o' riding. Like this one.' He bestowed a pat upon the little broomstick.

He seemed to take all the bewildering events so much for granted that Mary, afraid of seeming too ignorant,

bit back her questions and merely said, with caution:
'Yes, they do look newer, Mr – Mr Er?'

'Flanagan's the name. Danny Flanagan. I'll take it
kindly if you'd call me Danny. Newer, is it? Take a look
at that, now.'

He pointed to one bright new handle where a label
still hung which bore the legend, HARRODS.

'Newer, is it?' he demanded again, his voice cracking
with scorn. 'Made yesterday, that's what it is, and of
what? Not twigs, no, not good birch like a solid well-
bred besom. Not any more. All sorts of fancy stuff they're
using now, with the grand names to it, like you'll get
in Madam's labs. Nylon they call it.' He spat. '*Nylon*.
And three-speed gears. What next? What next, I ask
you? Engines, they'll be using next! See that paper on
the wall? Brought it with her last week, one o' them did.
Thought I'd be interested, she said. Interested! Take a
look at it!'

Mary took a look. The offending paper was a page
from a sales catalogue, which was tacked to the stable
wall. It carried a picture of a cheerful and very smart
lady sitting side-saddle on a complicated-looking pink
contraption, pouring steaming liquid from a coffee-pot
as she sailed through clouds like soapsuds. Above this
was printed, in big black letters: WITCHES! HARRODS
OFFER YOU THE HELIBROOM! Underneath, in smaller
letters, was a paragraph where Mary glimpsed the
phrases 'remote control . . . pastel colours . . . two-
stroke engine made of aluminium . . . matching telescope and coffee percolator . . .' And at the bottom, in
very small letters indeed: 'Price £874·75.'

'Well?' demanded Mr Flanagan. He was glaring

fiercely at Mary. She thought she had never seen such bright green eyes.

'It's awfully expensive,' she ventured.

He snorted. 'Even if I'd twice the money for a broom like that, d'ye think I'd ever be using it? Me? Me on a pastel-coloured ladies' ride with an aliminion engine? Helibroom!' The contempt in his voice was biting. 'Ye'd get me sooner on a feather mop, or one o' them new-fangled Hoovercraft. It's the likes o' them that's going to take the bread-and-butter out o' me mouth.'

'Oh?' said Mary, startled by this very normal remark. 'Do you have bread and butter here?'

Mr Flanagan stared. 'And why wouldn't we? Do you not have it, yourself? You must be coming from a quare place indeed not to be having that.'

'Oh, but we do. In fact, I've got some here. I brought a picnic lunch with me.' She took her lunch packet out of her pocket, and began to open it. 'Would you like a sandwich, Mr Flanagan?'

He shook his head. 'I'll be getting me own later. But you'd better eat yours now, there isn't much time. Come on out into the sun.' And before she could ask him what he had meant, he led the way out of the stable and shut the half-door behind them.

The sun was beautifully warm. Mr Flanagan went back to his old seat on the mounting-block, and patted the stone beside him, inviting Mary to sit. To her great relief (for until that moment she had forgotten all about him) Mary saw Tib there, sitting placidly in the sunshine, washing his face. She sat down beside Mr Flanagan and started to eat.

'Why did you say those new broomsticks would take

the bread-and-butter out of your mouth, Mr Flanagan?'

'Danny.'

'Why, then, Danny?'

'It's me job,' said Mr Flanagan simply. 'All me life I've taught riding. And I mean rale, genu-ine riding, that's not just pulling of levers and pushing of knobs, but how to stick on, whatever happens, in all the weathers, at all speeds – and how to be managing a bucking broomstick at a thousand feet or so on a moonless mid-night, with a storm coming up —' He nodded at Mary, his green eyes glittering. '*That's* riding,' he said. 'And not only that – it's knowing the words to use.'

'Like the words you said to my broom?'

'Them words is simple enough. They're the stopping words. But there's a lot to learn. And you, my girl,' said Mr Flanagan sternly, 'have a lot to learn, I'd say. I misremember seeing you before – how long have you been coming for lessons?'

'For lessons?' echoed Mary blankly. 'I – I've never been before. You mean *riding* lessons, on that broom-stick?'

'Fine I know you've had no riding lessons from me,' said Mr Flanagan. 'Or you'd not have been falling off at me feet the way you'd make a hole in the yard. No, it's the other lessons you'll be having at the College.'

'College?' echoed Mary again. 'What College?'

He pointed across the yard to where, under the clock-tower, the arched tunnel led from the stableyard out into the park. To one side of the archway was a notice fastened to the wall. Mary could read it quite easily from where she sat.

ENDOR COLLEGE
All Examinations Coached for by
A Competent Staff of Fully-
Qualified Witches.
Under the supervision of
MADAM MUMBLECHOOK, M.M., B.Sorc.,
Headmistress

'That's it,' said Mr Flanagan. 'That's the College, and one of the best of its kind. And now, if you've finished your lunch, you'd better be getting along. You don't want to be late for classes on your first day, do you now?'

'But I don't want —' Mary was interrupted by the sound of a bell, which came from somewhere inside the building.

'Hurry up!' cried Mr Flanagan, jumping off the mounting-block, and pulling her down after him. 'That's the first bell. It's three minutes you've got now, and they'll be looking for you.'

He took her by the arm and urged her towards the archway.

'But I'd much rather stay here and talk to you!' cried Mary, hanging back. 'I don't have to go in, do I? There's been some mistake – they're not really expecting me at all.'

'Sure and they are. Everybody knows you're here. Didn't you hear the alarm-cock?' As he hurried her forward, Mr Flanagan nodded to the bright weather-cock overhead. 'And it whirling round on its stick like it would be taking off for the moon or the gardens of Jerusalem? Come along now, me dear, don't be nervous. Your little cat's there already.'

And Mary saw that this, indeed, was true. Tib was ahead of them, trotting out of the archway into the sunlight of the park. He stopped and looked back. He looked alert and eager, as if this (thought poor Mary) was what he had been all along expecting to do.

'And that reminds me,' said Mr Flanagan at her elbow, 'don't be overlooking this, me dear. It's very strict they are, very strict indeed.' And he pointed to another small but forbidding notice which was fastened to the outer wall of the archway.

It said: '*Familiars not allowed in the park except on leash.*'

Mr Flanagan bobbed down like a diving duck and came up with an indignant Tib. 'Have ye got a lead?'

'No, I haven't. And besides, that's not a familiar, that's Tib.'

'Not a familiar? Black as he is, and with the eyes on him like emeralds? You'll be telling me next you're not a witch, and fine we both know that you'd never have got that broomstick this far, and you with no lessons either, unless you knew the words. Quick, now, there's the other bell. Tie some string on him, and get away in. Hurry!'

His haste was so catching, and her own bewilderment so great, that almost without thinking Mary put her hand in her coat pocket, and brought out a length of old Zebedee's raffia. On this Mr Flanagan pounced with a sound of satisfaction, and, before she knew exactly what was happening, Mary found herself walking across a wide gravel sweep towards the great door of the house with one end of the raffia clutched tightly in her hand, and Tib – rather offended and very dignified – stalking ahead of her with the other end loosely tied round his

neck. The air was very still, and very quiet. Not a single
bird, not one, was singing in the trees.

And now they were at the foot of the wide flight of
steps that led up to the front door. There were griffins
here, too. They sat on their stone pedestals, one at each
side of the steps. On the right-hand pedestal Mary saw
yet another notice. It said, simply:

TRESPASSERS

WILL BE

TRANSFORMED

Mary stared, stopped dead, then turned quickly to
look behind her.

Mr Flanagan was nowhere to be seen. And as he went
back to his stableyard, he had shut the gate behind him.
The archway was barred by a solid slab of studded oak.

Then the front door of the College opened, and a tall
woman in black came out on to the head of the steps.
She beckoned to Mary.

Mary looked at Tib. Tib looked back with no expression whatever in his green, green eyes.

The woman beckoned again.

Mary walked up the steps towards her.

TRESPASSERS
WILL BE
TRANSFORMED

THE woman on the steps was tall and handsome. She
had black hair, wound into a big bun on the nape of
her neck, and the skirt of her long black dress swept the
ground. And she wore diamonds. Lots of diamonds.
Rings, pendants, brooches, and earrings as big as dog-
daisies. Mary thought that she must be a queen, or at
least a duchess, but it seemed as if Mr Flanagan and the
notices had told the truth, for the woman smiled
pleasantly down at Mary, and said:

'I am the Headmistress, Madam Mumblechook. You
may call me Madam.'

'Thank you,' said Mary politely, holding on tightly
to Tib's leash.

'Welcome,' said Madam Mumblechook in a deep
carrying voice, 'to Endor College.'

'Thank you,' said Mary again, 'but I'm not quite
sure —'

'You are, of course,' said the Headmistress, with a
piercing look, 'a new pupil? When I saw you approach
with your familiar —' she waved at Tib — 'I realised at

once that you were to be one of us. Not,' she added
thoughtfully, 'a Trespasser?'

It was, Mary remembered, rather dangerous here-
abouts to be a Trespasser. One was Transformed.
And she had no intention whatever of being Transformed.

She said firmly, 'I'm a new pupil, Madam, thank
you.'

'Excellent, excellent. I'm sure you'll do well, and be
very happy with us.'

The Headmistress turned and led the way into the
building. There was a wide entrance hall, and to the
left of this a door stood open on what was apparently an
office. Mary could see a big desk, a shelf for books, and
filing cabinets against the wall. On the door was painted,
in black, the word HEADMISTRESS. It was comfortingly
normal.

Madam Mumblechook paused by the office door.
'Let me see now, are you boarding with us, or studying
as a day pupil?'

'A day pupil, please,' said Mary quickly.

'Ah, just so. Well, we must decide which grade to
start you in, then you can be duly enrolled. What is your
name, my dear?'

'Mary Smith.'

Madam Mumblechook looked at her thoughtfully.
'Yes, of course. It always is. You are the sixty-third, I
think. Or is it sixty-fourth?'

'Sixty-fourth what?' asked Mary, startled.

'The sixty-fourth Mary Smith,' said Madam Mumblechook. 'Most witches like to study under an alias, and
they like to choose the best name for it. Of course if we

ever got anyone who really *was* called Mary Smith . . .
But never mind that now. Come and see the classrooms,
and then we can discuss which courses to enrol you
for.'

From the rear of the hallway two corridors led off to
left and right. Madam Mumblechook turned to the right.
'The other way leads to the boarders' wing,' she said,
and Mary remembered the low, new-looking buildings
she had glimpsed from the air. 'The classrooms and
laboratories are down this way. Come, Miss – er –
Smith.'

'But my name is *really* Mary Smith!' cried Mary,
hurrying after her down a long corridor swimming in
dim-green shadow. The Headmistress did not seem to
have heard her. She was opening the door into what
appeared to be a classroom.

But it was not like any classroom that Mary had ever
seen or even imagined. For one thing, it was dark – so
dark that at first Mary could hardly make out the faces
of the pupils who sat in the desks below the teacher's
dais. Also it was small; there were only seven pupils. The
light – what there was of it – came from a single candle,
which burned with a bright green flame, and made the
face of the teacher, who leaned over it, look very
peculiar indeed.

The teacher was an old man who appeared – such was
the curious light – to have green eyes, green hair and
beard, and green skin. He looked very much as Mary had
always imagined a merman would look, only older,
greener, and – it must be admitted – much less whole-
some, like something going mouldy. He sat tapping a
long, clawed finger on the table in front of him, keeping

time to the chanting of the pupils in those dimly seen desks.

At first it sounded like children chanting nursery rhymes, or even their tables, as Mary knew they had done in infant schools many years ago, when her grandmother was a girl. In keeping with the candle-light, Mary thought, and Madam's long black dress and old-fashioned hairdo. But then she saw that the pupils were not children at all. Dimly, by the queer candle-light, she saw them, disembodied faces swimming green in the shadows; two old ladies, an elderly man with a round, dimpled face, three more ladies rather younger, and a seventh pupil whom she took at first glance to be a child, till she saw he was a dwarf, and quite middle-aged at that. And they were all chanting, not the ordinary nursery rhymes that Mary knew, but strange ones which went wrong here and there. It was as if the rhyme started out properly and then slipped somehow, so that the result was not ordinary, or even nice at all.

> Take a crooked sixpence,
> Crawl a crooked mile,
> Lay it in the moonlight
> On a crooked stile;
> Get a crooked cat
> To catch a crooked mouse,
> And lock 'em up for ever
> In a little crooked house.

It must, Mary realised, be a spell or charm – but what kind of magic could this be for? Nothing, surely, to do with the flying broomstick and Tib, and the beautiful fly-by-night flower?

One two three four
Mary's at the College door;
Five six seven eight
Let her in and it's too late . . .

The chanting wavered and died away as she and Madam Mumblechook stood in the doorway. Eight pairs of eyes – all apparently green – were fixed on her. She felt a little frightened, but then a soft touch on her leg made her remember Tib, and she bent quickly to caress his fur. It was ruffled, as if he were excited or apprehensive too; but it was silky and real and comforting.

'This,' said Madam, 'is the first grade Arts class. Spells of the simpler kind. Turning milk sour, blighting turnips, making the cows go dry. In the second term we progress further to such things as cramps, aches, and agues. The third term is devoted to revision and field work, and the examinations are in December.' She paused. 'And the College has its recreations too. Midnight picnics – though these are usually only for the boarders; and of course flying lessons. The aerial gymkhana is in the summer term. And that reminds me, my dear – there is no need to fly in past the stableyard; it upsets the alarm-cock. You may have noticed our private landing strip on the north turret.'

'I believe I did,' said Mary.

'Then come in that way, next time. Of course all our pupils, day pupils and all, are expected to attend our annual congress in the Harz Mountains on April 30th.'

Mary did not quite know what to say, but the Head-

mistress did not wait for an answer. She signed to the old
man on the dais and the chanting began again:

> Ding Dong Bell,
> Pussy's in the well;
> She wouldn't have gone right in
> But oh, but oh, she's terrible terrible thin . . .

Mary bent down quickly and touched Tib again, then
raised her voice across the chanting:

'You said something about laboratories, Madam. Do
you have science courses?'

'Yes, indeed. We hold Advanced Study courses under
one of the most distinguished of wizards, Doctor Dee.
You will have heard of him. But have you reached science
studies yet? You look very young.'

'My father is a scientist,' said Mary. 'A professor.'

Madam raised her brows. 'Indeed? Where, may I
ask?'

'Cambridge.' Mary had to shout to make herself
heard through a very noisy spell about warts.

> One, two, spotty ma coo,
> Three, four, slick as a doo;
> Warty, warty, jiminy jane,
> Up the chimbley and back again . . .

Now Madam looked definitely impressed. She led the
way out of the classroom, and the door closed on the
chanting. 'Gormbridge? Then he must be a warlock of
the very highest order. No wonder you are advanced for
your age, Miss Smith. He has taught you himself?'

'Well,' said Mary, 'not really, except that he taught

me to read before I went to school. And of course I knew all those rhymes when I was very little – only they weren't quite the same.'

'A different version? How very interesting. These regional variations can be most instructive. We must collate, my dear Miss Smith, we must collate. And your mother? No doubt she, too, is accomplished?'

'Oh, yes. She was at Cambridge, too. She was one of Daddy's students.'

'Really! So there is talent on both sides! Indeed we shall be happy to welcome you to Endor. A most promising recruit. Where are your parents now?'

'They're abroad, so they sent me to stay in the country for a while.'

'And they sent you to me. I am flattered, very flattered indeed. Of course we shall enrol you immediately. You must begin classes today. What grade were you in at Gormbridge?'

'The third form.'

'The *third?* Then no doubt you have already studied some of the more difficult spells. You will already be well beyond our first grade.'

'Blighting turnips and things? We don't use spells for that kind of thing now,' said Mary, who was beginning to enjoy herself. 'We use sprays.'

'Methods change, methods change,' said Madam, 'but basically magic remains the same. One can do a tremendous amount of damage in a very short time, if one gets the ingredients right. Have you studied invisibility yet?'

'No,' said Mary, 'but I should like to, very much.'

This was true. It seemed that she was going to keep

her end up well enough with the Headmistress, so she might as well enjoy the adventure, and bluff the day through, and no doubt at the end of it would get the little broomstick to carry her home again.

But, she thought, remembering the weird green candle, and the moist eyes of the chanting pupils, and the nasty little songs they sang, she would never come back. Never. It might be exciting, and interesting, and quite harmless, but – she realised suddenly – she would rather be back at Red Manor, all alone, sweeping up the leaves on the autumn lawn.

Madam Mumblechook opened another classroom door.

'Second grade. The invisibility class,' she announced.

This classroom was quite different, and looked much more normal. It was big, and had enormous windows through which the sunlight blazed. There was a dais with a long table for the teacher, and behind this a blackboard – a red blackboard, with writing on it in yellow chalk. And there were rows of desks in front, about thirty all told. The room was deserted.

Mary was just about to ask where everyone was, when Madam Mumblechook said with obvious satisfaction, 'Ah, I see the class is going very well. A hundred per cent. Very satisfactory. A good formula, obviously. Would you care to try it, Miss Smith?'

She pointed to the writing on the blackboard. This was spidery and not very easy to read, being written from corner to corner of the blackboard, instead of straight across. It was, moreover, in a foreign language.

Mary's new-found confidence ebbed abruptly. 'I – I'm not sure that I would, at the moment, thank you,' she said. Again she was just about to ask where the class was, when something began to happen that was stranger than anything she had yet seen.

Right in front of her, where there had been nothing but the empty dais and behind it the red blackboard – redboard, surely, thought Mary – someone seemed to be standing. A shadow only at first, a sort of ghostly outline of a person in front of the sunshine. There was no colour, only shape, and a sort of shimmer of personality, which slowly gathered substance till it became a smile on the face of a pleasant-looking man. Then all at once he was fully there, standing on the dais with one hand resting on a book which lay open on the table. In his other hand was a thin white stick, which Mary realised must be a wand. From time to time it hissed faintly, and green sparks spurted or dripped from its tip like drops from a leaking tap.

'Doctor Dee,' said the Headmistress, 'this is Miss Mary Smith. She is to enrol with us, and I feel sure that she will become one of our most able scholars. She is already adept at many of the elementary branches of magic. Her parents both studied – *both* of them, Doctor Dee – at Gormbridge.'

'What a splendid start!' said Doctor Dee, his eyes twinkling at Mary. 'And what a splendid name. How do you do, Miss Mary Smith?'

'How do you do?' said Mary. 'Actually, you know,' she added, 'it isn't Gormbridge; it's Cambridge.'

'These local differences of pronunciation . . .' Madam, scanning the empty classroom, was hardly attending. 'So interesting. Ah! Doctor Dee!'

The Doctor, following her gaze, started, stared, and

then cried out, 'You, and you . . . *and* you, Grizel – keep your mind on your work! Concentrate! I distinctly saw you, all three of you!'

The classroom shone in the sunlight, bright and swept and empty, but Mary thought that, just as he spoke, she had seen, faintly shimmering at three of the desks in the back row, the seated figures of girls – women? – dressed in long loose robes like dressing-gowns, and each holding in her cupped hands what looked like a ball of glass. Then they were gone into the empty sunlight.

'Can you read it?' asked Doctor Dee. He pointed at the formula on the redboard with his wand. The green sparks fizzed, and the yellow words danced up and down like gnats in sunlight. 'Oh dear, oh dear, I forgot to turn the power off. There, that's better, they're steady now. I know my writing is not always clear, but I hope that perhaps you can make it out. It's one of my own spells,' he added, wistfully, 'and some of my pupils find it much simpler than the classical ones.'

'It's very clear,' said Mary, not quite truthfully, but wanting to be polite.

'Really? Really?' He looked delighted. 'I know it isn't so foolproof as, say, the old Merlin formula or Professor Faust's; but one must move with the times, and some of the new fabrics proved resistant to the old formulae. You can shift velvet with almost anything, but the poly-amido synthetics and some of the acetate derivatives are the very angel to disintegrate.'

'I'm wearing a lot of nylon myself,' said Mary.

Rashly, as it happened. Doctor Dee beamed. 'Really? Then by all means let us try immediately! Here, hold this. I haven't a spare globe, but this will do.' He handed her a big glass ink-well that had been standing on the table. It was three-quarters full of ink. She hesitated, but Madam was nodding and smiling, and Doctor Dee's eyes shone with enthusiasm. Well, thought Mary, why not? She took it obediently between her hands. She could feel her palm still faintly sticky with the fly-by-night.

'Now,' said Doctor Dee, 'you know what to do. Read the words slowly and clearly, then watch the ink, and concentrate. You will soon see yourself going. Nylon or no nylon, I am sure that a young adept like yourself will have no difficulty whatever.'

Mary lifted the ink-well, and as she did so felt on her wrist the slight tug of old Zebedee's raffia, which was still attached to Tib's neck. She noticed that Tib was sitting at the edge of the dais, staring at the empty seats behind the empty desks, and his fur was brushed up. He took no notice of Mary.

'Can he see them?' she asked.

'Cats can see everything. This is what makes them so especially valuable to us,' said Doctor Dee. 'And of all the familiars – toads, owls, bats – a black cat with green eyes is the one that bears away the bell. And this one – the phoenix, the very pink or chrysolite of cats, I have no doubt?'

'Oh, yes,' said Mary. She would look the words up, she decided, when she got home, but Doctor Dee's drift was obvious. He was smiling down at Tib in obvious admiration.

'We do not often get a totally black cat. Splendid, splendid. Now, better give me the lead, Miss Smith. If he pulls at your hand and breaks your concentration, you will see nothing. I mean, you will see *something*, and that would never do!' Laughing gently at his own joke, he took the raffia out of Mary's hand, then pointed with the wand of power at the writing on the redboard.

'Now, Miss Smith of Gormbridge, we shall see – or not see!'

CHAPTER VII

Hinx, minx, the old witch winks,
The fat begins to fry . . .

IN the end, she managed very well. Doctor Dee read
the words with her. Afterwards she tried to remember
what they were, but never could. As soon as the last one
was said she bent her head and stared into the ink.

At first it was simply ink, a glossy, dark blue pool,
convex at the edges as if ready to brim over. On its
surface was a kind of skin where dust floated, as if the ink
were not liquid at all, but solid as glass. And, just as in a
glass, there was the room reflected, but very small, and
perfect in detail, like a miniature painting. She could see
the brilliant windows showing like tiny curved strips of
light, the painted walls, the redboard, and against them
her own reflection, made as small as they by the curved
surface of the ink. She stared, taking it in detail by detail,
the face she had studied so solemnly yesterday in the
mirror at Red Manor, wishing that something would
happen . . .

It was happening now. The little figure in the ink
was growing brighter, but behind it the reflected room

seemed to blur, its colours running and dissolving like a film going out of focus. The picture shook, blurred, faded, then dwindled down, down, down, to be lost in the darkness at the bottom of the well-shaft. For this was what the ink-well seemed now to have become. Mary found herself leaning over a deep well-shaft, her hands gripping the parapet, gazing into black depths where, still, her own reflection glimmered in a swirl of smoking darkness.

Then, as softly as a candle melting, and much more quickly, the tiny image slithered into shapelessness, whirled for a moment in smoke, and vanished . . .

Something stung her leg, a sharp, jabbing pain which made her jump. It must have shaken her back out of the spell, for faintly now through the swirling smoke she could see the classroom windows, and faintly hear, like something echoing in a well, the wizard's bland voice saying: 'Splendid! Splendid! Let's come back, shall we?'

He began to repeat a formula – not the same, but the words sounded familiar, and soon she realised that it was the original one spoken in reverse. And, in the ink, the spell reversed. Her face reappeared against the dark, gathered shape and colour as it swam closer against the sunlit background of the room, then it was only her reflection, small in a pool of ink.

She looked up, blinking in the sunlight. The Head-mistress was looking pleased, and here and there in the classroom a few pupils had reappeared unrebuked, and were watching with interest.

Doctor Dee was smiling. 'That was excellent. Remark-able for a first time, remarkable. But of course the

Gormbridge background is bound to tell, eh? Next time you will be able to do it yourself, but I think we should leave it at that for the present. One shouldn't go in for long, the first spell of the term. Now I am sure Madam Mumblechook wants to show you the other classes.'

He pushed Tib's lead into Mary's hand. As she went out into the dim corridor with the Headmistress, Mary could hear him beginning to scold the pupils who had reappeared.

'This way,' said Madam Mumblechook. 'I think you will find it interesting. It's the Science Practical, which I'm conducting myself. The teacher is unavoidably absent.'

'Is she ill?'

'You might say so. She made a slight mistake with the spell. Always a tricky thing to do with the advanced classes. Complete accuracy is, of course, essential. Here we are.' She opened the door. 'Why, what is it, Miss Smith?'

As light from the opened door streamed into the corridor Mary had stopped, and was staring down at Tib. Or rather, at where she had imagined Tib to be. The end of the raffia was in her hand, as Doctor Dee had given it back to her, and she thought she had felt Tib gently tugging at the collar, but he was not there. Only the collar dangling . . . No, she realised, not dangling, but floating along beside her, for all the world as if the little cat were still inside it. But she could not see him.

'Tib!' she cried. 'My cat! I know he was beside me all the time, because he scratched my leg to bring me back out of the spell. I must have left him —'

'You haven't left him.' Madam Mumblechook's voice

was amused and unperturbed. 'He's still there. Stroke him and see.'

Mary stooped and reached out, and there, indeed, was the warm fur and the strong, soft body of the cat. His head was smooth under her hand, the ears tucked back flat, and she could feel the thickness of the brushed-up fur. His whole body vibrated faintly, like something thrilling with an electric shock. He did not purr.

As she picked him up, he spat.

'Where are you going?' asked Madam, rather sharply.

'Back to Doctor Dee. The spell must have worked on Tib as well, but there must have been something wrong with the antidote, at any rate for cats. He'll have to bring him back.'

Madam Mumblechook laughed. 'Didn't you realise, child, that anyone can come back from that state at will? You did, didn't you? And you saw what happened to the people in class when they stopped concentrating. Cats are familiar enough with magic, on the whole. Your Tib will come back when he wants to, and not before. Can't you feel how excited he is? Put him down now, or you'll make it harder for him. You heard him spit when you picked him up . . . That's right. Now come in, and I'll show you something really interesting. This is the class I think you should enrol in tomorrow.'

The third classroom was different yet again, and of a kind familiar to Mary. It was a laboratory. There were long benches with taps and basins, and racks of flasks and test tubes, and burners lit with the familiar green flame. Some dozen or so students in black coats bent over their work. On the bench nearest the door was a com-plicated apparatus where a girl not much older than

Mary seemed to be stewing various roots in a blue liquid which gave off a heavy, sweet smell. She was stirring the mixture with a long whitish rod shaped like a bone. At the next bench a young man, with one eye bent to a microscope, scribbled notes in a thick, yellow book. There was a cage of mice on the bench beside him. Someone else was running a thick green liquid over some very beautiful white crystals in a bowl. From this a sharp violet-coloured smoke came off with a hiss and a smell of burning hair. At the far end of the long room a furnace burned green behind its transparent door. The laboratory windows were small and barred, and set high in the walls. Mary noticed how the light outside had changed; she must have been under the invisibility spell for far longer than she had realised.

'I must see how my students are getting on,' said the Headmistress. 'Sit down here and wait for me. I won't be long. Classes are almost over for the day.'

Mary obeyed her, sitting down in the chair behind the teacher's desk. She could feel Tib close beside her leg, but when she bent to stroke him he spat again, and she drew back. She sat quietly, looking round the lab which was so familiar and yet so strange – weird even – and found herself wishing uneasily that Madam Mumblechook would hurry up and dismiss the class, then enrol her for tomorrow, and let her go.

Madam Mumblechook went slowly from bench to bench, talking to the students, bending over their work, and sometimes sitting beside them to discuss it. Once or twice Mary had been in her father's laboratory, and had seen him doing almost the same things. But that room had been light and clean, smelling of polish and clean

chemicals and sunshine. This smelt queer, fusty, unpleasant almost, like a room which has been dark and
locked too long.

Madam's voice talked softly on at the far side of the
room. Liquids dripped and trickled, the mice scrabbled
and squeaked in their cage. The furnace roared. A big
clock ticked, a slightly uneven sound. The lead weights
were shaped like mice. The pendulum swung to and fro,
to and fro, tick tock, tick tock . . .

> Hickory dickory dock
> The mouse ran up the clock
> The mouse was dead
> As a lump of lead
> And rock, rock, rock in the clock,
> Rickety rock said the clock . . .

Mary shook herself awake. Now, outside the high
windows, she could see the light was fading fast. The
clock said ten minutes to six. Surely the class must be
over soon? Great-Aunt Charlotte and Miss Marjoribanks
would be home in half an hour, and Mary ought to be
there before that, or there might be questions asked
which certainly she would find it difficult to answer.
Mary decided to give Madam till six o'clock, then
announce firmly that she must go.

On the teacher's desk in front of her was a pile of
papers held down by a glass weight shaped like a frog.
Light from the burners glittered on it, till it seemed to be
staring at Mary with green, jewelled eyes. Beside it a
pen – an old-fashioned quill pen made of a grey goose
feather – stuck upright in a pewter inkstand. There was
a ruler marked in scribbly characters which might have

been Greek, or Arabic, or just simply Spider. Then a
cube, with strange marks on the faces. A triangle made of
worn brass, engraved with a mermaid.

Idly, she glanced at the papers, then with more
interest, as she saw that they were drawings of animals.
She lifted the glass frog off the pile, and began to
examine them.

They were certainly animals, but not any animals
that she had ever seen. There was one she thought at
first was a squirrel, until she saw it only had two legs,
and a thin tail like a rat's. Then there was a bird with no
feathers, not even on its wings. Then something that
might have been a hedgehog, except that it had no
eyes and nose, which made it look like a sea urchin with
feet.

It was like the nursery rhymes. Each one seemed to
start out right, then go suddenly, terribly wrong. Mary
hated them. She pushed them back under the glass frog,
and looked at the clock. Five minutes to go. Madam
Mumblechook was still talking, but work seemed to be
finishing. One of the students was turning out the
flame under a bubbling flask, and another had gone to a
sink to wash out some apparatus. The young man with
the microscope had put away his work, and now brought
the book across to the desk where Mary sat, and put it
with some others on a shelf beside her. Then he went out,
and some of the other students with him.

Mary glanced at the book. It was just called *Notes*,
which did not seem interesting, and the thick brown one
beside it was called *Metastasis*, and was by somebody of
the name of Dousterswivel. Mary decided not to read it.
But the next looked more promising; it was bound in a

soft dark red, and had a cat most beautifully embossed in gold on the spine. It looked very old. Mary pulled it out of the shelf, and examined it under cover of the desk.

The cat was on the front cover as well, with the title of the book going round it in a circle like the lettering on a coin. The title was, apparently: *Mafter fpells*.

She opened it. The paper inside was thick and supple, almost like skin, with wavy edges. On the fly-leaf was written in a large, flowing hand which she was sure was Madam Mumblechook's: *For fenior ftudents only. Not to be taken away.*

Once, in an old book Daddy had been studying, Mary had seen s's that looked like this. So *that* meant . . . She looked at the cover again. Yes, it made sense now. The book was called *Master Spells*. She opened it.

The pages were printed in the curious old print that she had seen in Daddy's book. Here and there were diagrams, like geometry, only not the same; curious arrangements of circles and triangles, and shapes she couldn't put a name to.

Then her eye caught one of the headings:

How to Choofe fubjects for Tranfformation.

On the page opposite this was one much simpler:

To Unfaften Locks.

And *that*, thought Mary, might be very useful, if Tib and I are to get out of here. Even to herself she did not like to admit that now she was very uneasy indeed. And Tib was uneasy, too, she was sure: even if he had, in a sense, brought her here – or arranged for her to come –

and had seemed excited about it, why did he insist now on staying invisible?

The last of the students was packing up. Mary hesitated, then quietly slipped the red book into her pocket.

The clock checked, whirred, and struck six. Madam Mumblechook came smiling down the length of the room, her diamonds glittering green in the dusk against the light of the flames.

'AND now, my dear,' said Madam Mumblechook, 'classes are over for the day. If you will come to my office and put your name down, I shall give you a prospectus, and we shall expect you in the morning.'

Mary got to her feet, relieved, and half ashamed of her fear. The book weighed heavy in her pocket. She put a hand down, hoping to slip it back unnoticed into its place, but Madam Mumblechook came swiftly round the desk to pause right beside the bookshelf – and it was too late.

'My books,' the Headmistress was saying, swooping on them with a rustle of the black robes. 'If you will just give me a moment, I will lock my books away. At night they go in the strong-room. None of them leaves this room. I'm sure you understand why, Miss Smith.' And she took the dozen or so books from the shelf and made for a door that Mary had not noticed, right behind the teacher's chair.

'Madam Mumblechook—' began Mary guiltily.

'One moment,' said Madam. 'Silence, if you please.'

Mary stopped. Madam Mumblechook, with the pile of books held against her chest, was facing the strong-room door, and chanting something very softly under her breath. Mary could not hear the words. There seemed to be no lock or key on the door, only a bronze handle shaped like a sea-horse. Madam laid hold of this and pulled. There was a series of clicks, smooth and oiled, and the door began to swing open. It was a huge, heavy door, made of metal, and at least nine inches thick. To Mary's surprise there was a light inside the strong-room; not green this time, but a dim, ordinary yellow, like an oil lamp. Madam Mumblechook left the door standing wide, and went in with the books.

'Would you be so good, Miss Smith, as to bring the papers off my desk?' she called. 'And the paperweight as well, of course. I always lock him up at night, along with the others. One can hardly be too careful, can one?' And she gave a little chuckling laugh.

It was Mary's chance. She pulled the red book from her pocket, picked up the pile of papers and put them on top of it, then carried the whole lot, with the glass frog, into the strong-room.

And the strange thing was that Tib ran ahead of her, pulling eagerly on the raffia lead.

There was a big cupboard just inside the door, and in this Madam Mumblechook was stacking the books.

'I suppose you want this as well,' began Mary. 'I was just looking—' Then she stopped dead, with a gasp. She had seen what else the strong-room contained.

To begin with, it was a far bigger room than she had thought. It was almost as big as the lab, and the soft light of the lamp near the door had only illumined the end of it, leaving the rest in shadow.

Mercifully in shadow. The whole of the long, dim room was lined from floor to ceiling with cages. They were barred and meshed, and stacked on one another like the shelves in a huge library, and there were bays where other ranks of cages stuck out from the wall. Some of the cages – those nearest the door – were empty, but from those further back in the shadows peered eyes, the eyes of small creatures, silent and staring, caught by the lamplight. Here and there was a movement as a paw or a tiny foot reached through the bars, but mostly the little creatures, whatever they were, sat huddled and silent in the dark corners at the back of their prisons.

Madam Mumblechook turned at Mary's gasp. 'Interesting, is it not? I thought you would be impressed. Some of our students have reached quite advanced experiments in transformation. But of course we have our failures.' She laughed merrily as she pointed at the nearest cage where a forlorn-looking creature, its orange fur patched with scales like mange, lay unheeding, its back to the room. It had put two crooked paws over its eyes to shut out the light, and seemed to be sleeping. But Mary suspected that it was very wide awake. She had already recognised one of the drawings from Madam's desk.

'Marvellous,' she said. Madam Mumblechook leaned over the cage, prodding irritably at the creature, which would not move. Without pausing to think why she did so, Mary slipped the red book of Master Spells back into her pocket. 'Here are your papers, Madam.'

'Ah, thank you.' Madam Mumblechook, abandoning the caged creature, thrust the papers and the glass frog into the cupboard and locked the door on them. She had not noticed the absence of the book. 'I will show you round in more detail tomorrow, my dear. But now you will want to be getting home.'

'Oh, yes, please!' Mary would never have thought she could be so thankful at the prospect of going back to Red Manor and Great-Aunt Charlotte. 'And I'd better hurry, Madam. They'll be missing me soon.'

'Then we shall hurry.' And the Headmistress moved quickly towards the strong-room door, her black robes rustling about her. Mary followed close on her heels, pulling Tib, who for some reason seemed reluctant to go with her. Then they were out in the lab, and behind them the strong-room door shut with a smooth *clunk*.

The lab was deserted now. The students had all gone. The burners were out. Only the furnace burned green and roaring.

Tib was still dragging at the lead. Mary stooped quickly and picked him up and held him tightly. This time he neither spat nor scratched, but she heard him growl deep in his throat, and she felt him still quivering with that queer tension and excitement. She followed Madam Mumblechook out of the lab and along the corridor.

The Headmistress's office was a pleasant, business-like place, and very ordinary, with shelves of books – quite ordinary books like *Who's Who*, and *What's What*, and *Teach Yourself Magic* – and a typewriter and a big desk. Mary stood restlessly near the door, hugging the invisible Tib, while Madam Mumblechook lifted a big ledger from a drawer and spread it open on the desk.

'Name? You still wish to go by the name of Mary Smith?'

Mary opened her mouth to protest yet again that it was her real name, then stopped. There was no point, after all, since she would not be coming back. 'Yes, please.'

The Headmistress was inscribing the name in that bold, flowing hand that Mary recognised. 'Very well. Mary Smith Sixty-four.' She was writing it, Mary noticed, as LXIV. Madam underlined this carefully. 'There. That is how you will be known among us. Address?'

'Red Manor, Shropshire.'

Madam glanced up at that, her eyes suddenly very piercing. 'Indeed?' She seemed to be about to say something further, but merely raised her brows, nodding, then turned back to the ledger. And now Mary, craning forward, could see what had surprised her. The previous entry looked almost exactly the same. It ran:

Mary Smith LXIII, Red Manor, Shropshire.

Madam closed the book with a snap. 'So that is that. Delighted to have you.' She dropped the book back in the drawer and handed Mary an envelope. 'Here is our prospectus. We will discuss fees later, but believe me, we shall be most grateful for your generous donation. So many prospective pupils have no idea that a little initial gift is not only very acceptable, but – shall we say? – an excellent start to one's college career. When you have had time to think it over, I am sure you will see it in this light.'

'I don't understand,' said Mary.

Madam smiled kindly. 'All in due course, my dear, all in due course. At the moment everything is so new

to you . . . Tomorrow at ten, then, and we shall discuss
your classes. A little distilling, I think, and some practice
with the astrolabe for instrument flying, but I think – I
really think – that your father's daughter can go straight
on to transformation.'

'Thank you,' said Mary. She was glad to hear that
she did not sound nervous, only slightly worried. 'And
now I really think I'd better hurry home, Madam. My
great-aunt likes me to be washed and changed by half
past six, and—'

'Badness me,' said Madam mildly, looking at the
clock on the wall, 'then certainly you must be going.
I'm afraid that our private landing strip is locked now,
except for residents, but Danny will have your broomstick ready at the door.'

And he had. He was waiting at the foot of the front
door steps in the thick dusk, holding the little broomstick,
which stood quite still in his grasp, just like an ordinary
broom. So like an ordinary broom that Mary, running
down the steps with relief in the fresh evening air, had a
moment's terrible doubt. Had this morning's journey
really been true? Had she really flown? And could she
fly again?

'Will it know the way?' she asked anxiously, and Mr
Flanagan grinned cheerily.

'It will that. They're each after having their own
runs, and this one will be getting you there with a lep
like a blooming grasshopper. If you can stay on, that is.
Come along then, me dear, I'll haul him the while
you'll be mounting. Be aisy, now, will you?' This to the
broomstick, which began to sidle and skip as Mary tried
to mount it.

'Let me hold the cat,' said Madam Mumblechook, and lifted Tib from Mary's arms. Tib was growling and grumbling audibly now, his voice rising to a squall as Madam Mumblechook busied herself tying the end of the raffia lead to the broom handle.

'Stand back, now!' cried Mr Flanagan. 'Hauld on, me dears!' And he gave the little broomstick a slap, and shouted: 'Home wid ye now!'

It did work. It was just the same, except that this time the broomstick tried no tricks, but rushed smoothly up into the air on a trajectory like a rocket. The birch twigs whistled in the air like a tiny jet engine. Then the broomstick curved out over the huge trees at the edge of the park, and fled for the last bright gap in the heavy clouds of evening with a speed that took Mary's breath from her lungs.

It had taken Tib's, too. As they left the ground with that tremendous leap, his squalling had checked as suddenly as if he had choked.

The clouds swirled round her, indigo and grey and aubergine, then suddenly golden, all smoke and flame and tossing fire. But this time she hardly noticed their beauty. She held on tightly to the broomstick, calling out to the silent Tib, and watching for the break in the sea of cloud which would mark the beginning of their descent.

Here it was. A great gap of darkness, like a lake of black water. The broomstick tore through the firelit surf of cloud at the edge of the gap, then plunged steeply down into the evening dusk above Red Manor.

It skimmed the top of the lime tree, and the autumn leaves, torn off in its wake, swirled round Mary's head

like a cloud of bats. There was a swish and tossing of
twigs, and the broomstick jerked once as if it had hit
something – or as if, thought Mary, clinging like a burr,
Tib had jumped clear into the lime boughs. And indeed,
when the broomstick ran to earth in a long wake of
blown leaves along the lawn, and she turned to look, the
raffia lead had gone, and no warm fur met her hand as
she stroked it along the twigs of the besom.

'Tib? Tib? Come down!' she called softly, dismount-
ing, and staring up into the twilit boughs of the big lime.
She could see the raffia lead, caught from some high
branch, swinging with the collar obviously empty. Tib
had pulled himself free, and, though surely not still
invisible, apparently was not yet ready to come to her.

Mary ran down the path towards the kitchen garden,
and put the little broomstick back in its place with a pat
of thanks. With a soft flirt of wings and a faint chirrup
the robin flew up on the wall by the tool-shed, and began
to sing. There were daisies all along the edge of the path,
and by the door as she ran in the evening primroses
shone pale and scented in the dusk. Everything was
normal and ordinary, and very comforting, and there in
the kitchen was Mrs McLeod just putting the pans on
the stove for supper.

'There you are. Did you have a good day, now?'

'Lovely, thank you,' said Mary. 'Is Aunt Charlotte
home yet?'

Mrs McLeod looked amused. 'You've beaten her,' she
said, 'but only just. I can hear the car there now. Run,
lassie.'

Nobody had asked any questions that could not be

answered. The old, old friend had apparently been good value, and Great-Aunt Charlotte and Miss Marjoribanks spent a happy supper-time talking about their day. For once, Mary was pleased that they seemed totally uninterested in hers.

At last she escaped up to her room. The first thing she did was to run across to the window and pull the curtains wide. Nothing but sky and stars. The clouds had cleared, and a fresh young wind tossed the lime boughs. There was no cat waiting on the window-sill.

She pushed the sash up and leaned out, calling softly. No reply.

Mary began slowly to undress, knitting her brows with worry. Supposing Madam Mumblechook were wrong, and Tib couldn't get his visibility back at will? Suppose the spell had been different from her own? Suppose – then she remembered the book, and put a hand in her pocket, half expecting the book to have vanished, too. But it was safely there, the embossed cat and the circle of lettering winking in the electric light.

Mary fingered it doubtfully. Not tonight, perhaps. No, this was something to be looked at tomorrow, when the sun was shining. Somehow, here in her own room, the book looked uneasily out of place, not belonging to the same world as the daisies, and the smell of the lime tree, and the robin's song. But there was Tib . . .

Well, Tib was probably all right anyway. Cats could cope with magic, they had told her. And in any case, Tib would have to be here himself for any kind of spell to work.

She put the book on her dressing-table, and then noticed, sticking out from between the pages where she must have pushed it, the envelope Madam Mumble-chook had given her with the College's prospectus. She picked it up. This was different; since she had no intention of ever going there again, it would be fun to have the prospectus to keep and read. Now that she was safely back at home, the adventure was pleasant enough to remember; apart from Tib's accident everything had gone well – and they thought she was a wizard's daughter . . .

Mary grinned to herself at the thought of Daddy making himself invisible. She would enjoy showing him the prospectus, and Mummy, too. How people would stare when they knew that there was a College for Witches, only a broomstick's ride away from Red Manor. She wondered if there was a picture, or even a map to show you how to get there. She opened the envelope.

A slip of paper fell out.

On it was written, in that big bold hand:

'Received with thanks of Miſs Mary Smith LXIV of Red Manor in Shropſhire, one Familiar for Tranſformation Experiments.'

And an initial below which looked like M.

CHAPTER IX

Can I get there by candle light?
Yes, and back again!
If your heels are nimble and light . . .

THERE was nothing for it. She would have to go back,
and tonight. They would hardly keep Tib unharmed
until tomorrow, when they expected Mary back as a
pupil, otherwise the Headmistress would not have been
so mysterious about the 'donation' Mary had made, and
she would have taken the little cat more openly, instead
of . . . Yes, thought Mary, as she hurried her clothes on
again, that was how they had done it. When Madam
Mumblechook took the cat from her she had simply
pretended to put him on the broomstick, then she had
tied the empty raffia to the handle, and Mr Flanagan had
sent the broomstick away before Mary had had time to
check on Tib's presence. They were all in it, nice
though they had seemed. And Doctor Dee, too – Mary
was sure now that he had deliberately left Tib invisible,
to help Madam and Mr Flanagan to snatch him. Cats
were 'especially valuable', Doctor Dee had said . . . But
if cats knew about magic, then Tib must have known

what he was risking. Why, then, had he deliberately led her to Endor College?

Mary stood in the middle of her bedroom, fully dressed again, thinking. It was quite dark outside, and the wind had grown stronger, and was roaring in the treetops. There were voices on the stairs now; Great-Aunt Charlotte coming to bed early, as usual. Miss Marjoribanks would be anything up to an hour later. It would be useless for Mary to attempt before that to creep downstairs unseen. She would have to wait.

She sat down in the chair by the lamp, and opened the red book called *Master spells*. Three spells, if they were there, she had to find. She found the index page and ran her finger down.

The first one she had seen before: *To Unfasten Locks.* The others would probably be more difficult – but surely there must be one to cancel invisibility, and one to undo a transformation?

But there was not. She started again at the top, and went down one by one, slowly. *To Change Into Stone. To turn Him Blue. To Strike Him Pink. To Render His Hands Powerless. To Transform Into Animals. To Transform One Animal Into Another* . . .

Mary's finger checked. The invisibility spell, she remembered, had been undone by being chanted backwards. Perhaps transformation spells worked the same way? She leafed through the thick yellow pages until she found the one headed *To Transform One Animal Into Another.* She skipped through the spell, which was gibberish, to the note at the bottom, which read, simply: '*This spell does not apply to cats, toads, or other familiar creatures of witches.*'

So it would not work. Cats were special. But since Madam had taken Tib for transforming, there must be a spell for it, and therefore there must surely be one to undo it. Unless – and it was possible – they never did undo transformations, just went on and on experimenting, changing one miserable shape into another . . .

It didn't bear thinking about. She went down the index again. Nothing, nothing . . . *ah!* She had it! At the foot of the page, printed small, was a star, and after it the simple words: *The Maſter ſpell.*

Mary turned to the back of the book.

There it was, printed in scarlet, with a star at the start of every line. And above it, under the heading *The Maſter ſpell,* was written in a small, crabbed hand: *To Undo any Magick within Range. This ſpell to be uſed only againſt Magick already made. If it is uſed where there has been no Magick, then it will come back upon the uſer, to his dire afflict-ion. Beware, and ſay me not ſave in ſore need.*

Mary read no further. Footsteps were coming creaking up the stairs. She switched the light off and waited, breathless in the dark, listening. She heard Miss Marjori-banks' door open and shut, softly. A few minutes later the grandfather clock in the hall struck eleven. The house settled, creak by creak, into silence.

At last she moved. She switched the light on and got into her dark coat and soft-soled shoes. She dropped a torch into one pocket and the book of spells into the other. She picked a head off the purple fly-by-night and kept it carefully in her hand.

Then, heart thumping, she opened her bedroom door.

It was quite quiet. The only sound was the steady ticking of the grandfather clock. The lights were out under Great-Aunt Charlotte's door and Miss Marjoribanks'. Mary switched on her torch and crept along the corridor to the stairhead, then slowly, slowly, down the stairs, avoiding the treacherous one three from the bottom, which creaked.

As she reached the hall the grandfather clock cleared its throat and struck the half hour.

Mary jumped. Then the steady, soft ticking started again.

Hickory dickory dock . . .

The memory came to her of that other clock, the one in the lab at Endor College, with the lead weights that looked like horrid little dead mice, and the nasty rhyme it seemed to click out. She shone her torch up at the grandfather clock. Its brass face winked at her. There were cherubs engraved in the upper corners, and between them a sun with curly rays all round a jolly face, cheek to cheek with a coy-looking moon. The weights were hidden in the clock-case, but Mary knew what they looked like; fir-cones, fat and tightly shut.

It was a lovely, old, homely clock, and it is possible that at that moment Mary would have gone straight upstairs again and tried to forget all about the other one, if a movement at the foot of the clock had not caught her eye. A mouse, a real one, small and glossy and bright-eyed, whisking aside out of the torchlight and vanishing into the wainscot.

'Wait till Tib sees you,' whispered Mary, and then said to herself, in surprise: 'And *that's* fair enough, it's the way things are; it's between Tib and the mouse.

But magic – magic isn't fair. Not on Tib *or* the mice – and not on those poor things in the cages, whatever they are. I'll have to go. And it wouldn't be right to use the spell-book to unlock the front door, either. I'll do it the way it's used to, even if it does take longer . . .'

It didn't take so very long. A few moments later the last bolt slid back and the key turned to let Mary out into the dark night air.

It was so easy that it was almost routine. The little broomstick was just where she had left it, and apparently it was asleep, because when Mary took hold of it, it gave a jump and a kick that nearly tore it out of her grasp. But now she knew what to do. She squeezed the fly-by-night in her hand, rubbed the hand down the broom-handle and said sharply: 'Stand still!'

The little broomstick stood still.

'That's better!' said Mary sternly. She settled torch and book carefully in her pockets, got astride the broomstick, stroked it – this time more gently – with the crushed flower, and commanded it:

'Endor College. Front door, and carefully, please!'

The broomstick, with only the tiniest quiver of a buck, leaped into the air and headed straight for the nearest bunch of stars.

It was impossible to tell distance this time, or height. The sensation of speed was, if anything, greater than during daylight, because all the stars seemed to be racing and wheeling as well. It was like flying through an enormous Catherine-wheel of a sky, where stars whirled and flashed, and the wake of the little broomstick fizzed with bubbles of light. Then the stars, pouring away, dwindled to bright dust, and the dusky trees sailed up and blotted them out, and the broomstick had arrived.

Just as it had been told. At the very foot of the front door steps.

Mary dismounted. The broomstick stood quite still for her, so as she propped it in the shadow of the house wall she gave it a friendly little pat and whispered, 'Wait for me, and be good. I won't be long.'

She stood for a moment in the shadow beside it, watching and listening. There were no lights in the windows. The alarm-cock was silent. Indeed, not many sounds would be audible above the rush of wind in the treetops. This had got stronger now, almost as if a storm were coming. Mary, flattening herself back into the deep shadow between the steps and the house wall, got out her book and her torch, and shone a cautious light on the page.

To Unfasten Locks . . .

It was right, she supposed, to use the spell on the front door of Endor College. It seemed such a simple little rhyme, but if the lock was indeed a magic one . . .

It was, and the spell worked. The door opened in smooth, obedient silence, and Mary, her heart thumping, stole into the hall. She shut the door quietly behind her and stood still, listening.

No lights; no sound. With stealthy flashes of her torch she tiptoed down the long corridor towards the door of the lab.

This was shut, but not locked. She eased it open, and was back in the horrid room she remembered. It was quite light. The furnace still roared green behind its transparent door, filling the long room with that phosphorescent decaying light, and striking gleams and ripples of glitter from the racks of jars and flasks.

The clock was ticking; off-beat it went, with its nasty little rhyme:

> Hickory dickory dock
> The mice got into the clock . . .

Mary ignored it. She shut the door carefully, and tiptoed past the teacher's desk to the massive, locked door of the strong-room.

The book was still open at the lock-spell. She put her hand, still faintly sticky with the fly-by-night, on the bronze sea-horse which did duty for a handle, and whispered the spell.

The huge door came smoothly open, and stood wide for her to enter.

Inside, the lamp still burned with its yellow light. Further back, in the dusk, the bars of the cages glimmered, and behind the bars, the eyes. All wide awake, all staring.

'Tib?' whispered Mary. 'Tib? Are you there?'

No answer. Only a rustling and a faint muttering, gobbling sound as all the queer misshapen creatures came crowding to the fronts of their cages. Those that had eyes had them fixed on her, beseeching. Small paws scrabbled at the bars.

'Tib?' Surely, if Tib were here, he would make some sign. She began to run along the rows of cages, peering in the faint light, calling, 'Tib? Tib? Tib?' in a desperate little whisper.

A squirrel shot a paw out and snatched at her sleeve, and she paused.

'Tib? Is that you?'

From the next cage a hedgehog's foot reached, urgently, and from the cage above a twisted claw stretched out to pat her hair.

Mary had not thought of this. She backed away from the wall of cages, and took out her torch again, sending its beam along the packed rows. 'Tib? Tib? If you're here, make a sound! Try, Tib! Try to mew! Surely you've still got a voice?'

But they all understood her. And they were all desperate. From every cage came small, frantic noises, as the rabbits, rats, squirrels, pangolins, hedgehogs, frogs and lizards tried, from all their differently shaped throats, to mew.

'Please, please—!' Mary, her hands to her ears, was almost crying. 'Can't you *understand*? I can't open all those locks; it would take hours and hours! And even if I could, how could you get away? You're all so little, and you've none of you got proper legs or wings! Please, *please* be quiet and let me find Tib!'

But they took no notice. The eyes besought her, the paws reached frantically through the bars, the little throats croaked and mewed and gobbled and cried.

Then suddenly, silence.

Then Mary, too, heard what they had heard. Footsteps were coming down the corridor towards the laboratory door.

CHAPTER X

Gay go up and gay go down

THERE were two sets of footsteps, and one of them belonged to Madam Mumblechook. Mary heard her talking, then a man's voice answering her.

She ran to the door of the strong-room, and stood there, listening. Perhaps they were not coming here; perhaps the voices would go straight past the laboratory door . . .

They stopped just outside it.

'A most successful experiment, Doctor Dee,' Madam was saying. 'And well worth staying late for. I believe we may congratulate ourselves.'

The doorknob turned.

Mary whisked back into the strong-room and pulled the massive door shut behind her. It closed quietly, with a faint gasp of air. She could hear nothing now. All round her the creatures were silent, save for the faint scratching of their feet on the floor of the cages, and their soft, hurried breathing. The air was dead; Mary heard her own heart as if it were footsteps.

They had spoken of an experiment. Perhaps they just wanted something from the lab. Perhaps they would not come in here . . .

She heard the lock of the strong-room door turn over with a smooth click.

When Madam Mumblechook and Doctor Dee came into the strong-room, Mary was at the far end of it, crouched on the floor in the darkness behind the last bay of cages.

'. . . in here,' Madam was saying, 'and that will do for tonight, I think? We can perhaps continue tomorrow?'

'Certainly,' said Doctor Dee. 'I admit to finding it a challenge, a real challenge. A more difficult subject even than the grey, wouldn't you agree?'

'Indeed. But how satisfactory to be able to check those results with this one, and so soon.' There was a sound of something being laid down. 'There. Quite a difference, isn't there? I don't think he'll be readily recognised now, even if she decides to be difficult about it.'

'All cats are grey in the dark, don't they say?' said Doctor Dee, and laughed. 'Ah, it's awake now. All is well. There was a moment, I admit to you, dear ma'am, when I thought I might have made the mixture too strong. But I venture to suggest that we may even be on the verge of discovering one of the classic formulae. I would not put it any less strongly. However, I suggest we leave the creature in the lab cage overnight, until – ah, naughty!'

Something had hissed, but not like a cat; like a snake, thought Mary. Madam Mumblechook laughed, and Doctor Dee said complacently, 'He'll learn. And now, dear Madam, I had better be on my way.'

'Come to my office first,' said Madam Mumblechook. 'One for the road. It's a wild night now, from the sound of the wind. Your broomstick is reliable?'

'Totally. Straight to its stable, and never a swerve to right or left. It's the only way it knows,' said Doctor Dee. 'After you, dear Madam.'

They were going. Mary held her breath. She had the impression that all the creatures in the cages held theirs. The great door whooshed shut on its cushion of air. Silence settled. She tiptoed out into the lamplight to see what Madam had brought.

In a small – a very small – cage made of bright, common-looking metal, a cage no bigger than a large mousetrap, sat a frog. It had a hunched back, protruding eyes, and a spotted skin. It was sitting up on its enormous haunches, and its forelegs were too short. They were just little curled claws, held tightly in to its chest. When it saw Mary, it hitched and shuffled itself forward on its haunches towards the bars, and tried to reach her with the tiny, useless paws.

An experiment, they had said. *A difficult subject. He'll learn*, they had said, and laughed.

Mary put a finger through the bars, and the little paws fastened round it. She saw how the lamplight ran over the freckled skin like silk; how the powerful frog-muscles bunched and glimmered; how the bulbous eyes shone.

'Tib?' she whispered. 'My pretty Tib. I know it's you. You'd be beautiful, whatever they did to you. And I think I'm beginning to understand; the "grey" they talked about, that was your brother Gib, wasn't it? He must be here too, somewhere. If I get you out, you can show me which he is, and we'll take him, too. Keep still, now, and let go my finger. I've got to find the Master Spell.'

For of course the lock-spell by itself would be useless. She must undo the transformation as well. She opened the book at the Master Spell.

The red lines, with their warning stars, seemed to quiver in the lamplight . . . *It will come back upon the uſer, to his dire affliction. Beware, and ſay me not ſave in ſore need.*

Well, this was sore need, and if it came back upon her, that was just too bad. It was already more than bad for Tib and his brother, and for these countless other creatures whom she wished so desperately that she could help as well.

She took a breath. The massive door was tightly shut. There was no need to whisper. She raised her voice to its normal pitch, and spoke quickly and clearly . . .

There were six lines of it, and it is not possible to quote it here, because never after this night was Mary able to remember a word of it. But it was a simple, gay little rhyme, and it ended on a phrase that might have been (but wasn't) 'the dancing ring of days.'

'. . . ring of days,' finished Mary, strongly.

That did it.

Everything happened at once.

With a clicking and a cracking like a million billion nuts popping under the feet of a hundred elephants, the locks of the cages – all the cages – flew open. The cupboard door fell off its hinges, and the glass frog rolled out as the books and papers on the shelves wisped away to charred ash. The strong-room door itself swung wide and stood. And out of every cage the creatures jumped, flapped, crept, shuffled, clawed their way, till they swarmed all round Mary's feet on the ground. Then, suddenly, the dim lamp swelled and flashed and sparkled, and the dead air of the strong-room went whirling and whistling through the bars of the empty cages and with it – instead of the grunting breaths and shuffling claws of the unhappy, stunted creatures on the floor – came the sound of wings and dancing hoofs. Under Mary's eyes a lame hedgehog stretched and grew and became a young deer, dappled and big-eyed, and supple as willow; a shuffling pangolin swept into the air with the knife-wings and scarlet throat of a swallow; the glass frog, rolling to her feet, melted into the steely velvet of a beautiful smoke-grey cat; then all round her were wings and the joyous cries of birds, and the light-flecked coats and tossing antlers of deer.

And from the little metal cage with its burst lock leaped Tib, eyes wide and brilliant, and landed on Mary's left shoulder, as the grey cat swarmed up her other arm to anchor every claw in the collar of her coat.

For a few shocked and deafened seconds Mary could not move. The sudden flashing magic, the appalling noise, seemed to split the night.

Then she shouted: 'Run, everyone! This way!' And tore out through the strong-room door and across the lab.

Here, too, was chaos. Tubes and retorts burst with cracks and flashes, and liquid ran down red, green, and purple, so that the deer's hoofs splashed coloured spray shoulder high as they galloped through. The clock weights dropped to the floor, became mice, and vanished down the nearest crevice, closely followed by the mice from the burst cage on the bench. The clock springs, released screaming, whipped up in great coils, whirled round and round three times, then smashed in a whirring tangle of metal.

'Hic,' said the clock, and stopped.

The furnace exploded.

The lab door stood wide. Mary, the book in her hand and the cats on her shoulders, dived through it and, with the air alive with birds and with a score of deer racing beside her, ran down the long corridor to the front door.

It was open, too.

But so was the door of Madam's office. And in that doorway, side by side, Madam Mumblechook and Doctor Dee stood transfixed and furious.

Then, together, they leaped into action. Doctor Dee whirled his wand of power up, and yelled, 'Stop! I bid you stop!' And Madam Mumblechook ran to slam the front door.

But nobody stopped, or even paused. Doctor Dee was waving his wand and shouting still, but his voice could not be heard for the noise of wings and hoofs and the excited calling of the animals and birds. Tib, on Mary's left shoulder, was yelling like a demon, and on her right, the grey cat answered. The noise was dreadful. And whether it simply drowned the wizard's voice, or whether the Master Spell still held, Madam and the Doctor were powerless. The front door sprang open against the witch's hands, so violently that she was flung back against the wall; and then the herd of deer, with Mary in their midst and the flock of birds sweeping overhead, ran clean over the wizard, knocking him, wand and all, flat to the floor. Then they were all racing anyhow down the wide steps and out in the fresh, free night.

The deer fled on, over the grassland, under the trees' shadow. Mary saw them reach the wall, and over it in the windy starlight they went like a lifting wave. The birds shot high into the starlit air, screaming with joy. Mary stumbled down the last step, the cats clinging like goosegrass, and ran for the dark corner where she had left her little broomstick.

It must have come to meet her. She almost fell over it, half-propped against the stone griffin at the foot of the steps.

She leaped astride it, clapped it with her hand, and shouted: 'Home! Straight home!'

It jumped into the air. As she soared over the trees, gaining height, she saw below her the last wave of deer leap the park wall and scud away into the dark woods. All around, the treetops were filled with birds, singing as if it were midday. Then woodland, birdsong, and the scent of the trees dropped away from her, and there was nothing but the flying starlight and the ecstatic shrilling of the two cats at her ears.

It seemed a much quicker ride than usual. The broomstick slowed, swooped down through a swirl of windy cloud, then coasted to a smooth landing on grass.

Mary dismounted stiffly. The cats leaped down off her shoulders, but, to her surprise, stayed close beside her feet, and even in the fitful light of the cloud-mantled stars she could see the arch of their backs, and the stiffness of their tails. They seemed to be staring at the house.

Mary turned to see what was scaring them so. Then she, too, stiffened and stood staring. And she knew that if she, like the cats, had had a tail, it would have been sticking straight up like theirs, and fluffy as a bottle-brush.

It was the wrong house.

She picked up the broomstick. Yes, it was the wrong broomstick, too. Her own little broomstick had, after all, stayed exactly where she had bidden it. And there had only been one other visitor to Endor College that night. 'Straight to its stable, and never a swerve to right or left,' Doctor Dee had said. And this was where it had brought her.

Mary stood there on Doctor Dee's front lawn, holding Doctor Dee's broomstick, and staring at the front of Doctor Dee's house with horror.

The cats spat, sprang away, and vanished into the shadows.

Someone jumped out of the bushes behind her. A voice said, gruffly and threateningly, 'So it was you, you rotten witch! Now I've got you, and you'd better do as I say!'

CHAPTER XI

Where she was going I couldn't but ask it,
For in her hand she carried a broom

IT was a boy; a boy of about Mary's own age,
perhaps a little older, but taller and tough-looking. His
hair looked quite dark in the starlight, and he was
scowling ferociously. He was also brandishing a thick
stick with a nasty-looking knob on the end.

Then he stopped, peered, and said on a note of
uncertain surprise, 'I know you, don't I? We've met
somewhere, but I don't remember – Who are you?'

Mary had backed a step in front of the threatening
cudgel. 'I've never seen you before in my life. I'm Mary
Smith, from Red Manor. Are you Doctor Dee's apprentice?'

'Doctor who's what? Of course I'm not!' He sounded
surprised and indignant, but he had let the cudgel fall.
'I'm the Vicar's son, Peter. I live in Redmanor too, but
I —' He took in his breath. 'Yes, that's it! I've seen you
in a photo up at the Manor, that's why I must have

thought I knew you. Daddy said you were staying with your great-aunt.'

'They told me you were away on holiday,' said Mary.

'We got back today. But look, what is all this? What are you doing here? And why should I be somebody's apprentice? Who's this Doctor Dee?'

'Don't you know? This is his house – at least, I think it must be.' He was scowling at her still, but uncertainly, and this gave Mary confidence. She added, 'What are you doing here yourself, anyway?'

'I came to look for my cat,' said Peter.

'So it is yours!' cried Mary. 'The grey one? It is Gib, then?'

He nodded. 'When we got back, Mr Spenser said Gib had disappeared a week ago, and they hadn't seen him since. We've looked everywhere, all day. Mother and Daddy said he must have gone astray, but I knew he would never do that. Then I found a note under one of the plant-pots in the potting shed. It said —'

'I know what it said. It was a receipt for "one Familiar for Transformation Experiments",' said Mary.

The boy stiffened, and the cudgel moved again as his grip tightened. 'Then you *are* a witch? I – I didn't think they were real, but when I saw you . . . I'm certain I saw you come flying in over that wall, and there's the broomstick to prove it! And I suppose this Doctor Dee of yours is a wizard as well, if you thought I was his apprentice!' He swung the cudgel up, and took a step forward. 'I promise you, if you don't give me my cat back—'

'Please,' said Mary, backing again, 'I'm not a witch, honestly! I just got mixed up in it, the same as you, because *my* cat disappeared as well, and as a matter of fact I've found them both, and transformed them back again. I found a book of spells, and —'

'Do you expect me to believe that?' demanded Peter. 'Where are they, then?'

'There,' said Mary, with relief, as the two cats, their fur once more sleek and shining, strolled out of the shadows on to the grass.

'Gib!' said Peter. The cudgel thudded down on the grass, and he snatched the cat up, hugging him. 'Where did you find him?'

'Look,' said Mary earnestly, 'there isn't time to tell you all about it. You'll just have to believe me, and I think we'd better be getting out of here now, this minute. There are two of them in it – Doctor Dee, and a witch who lives not far from here, and I think they may be coming after me. They're dangerous, I don't have to tell you.' She stooped and picked Tib up. 'So let's hurry, shall we? I'll tell you all about it on the way.'

But the boy didn't move. 'That's the whole point,' he said. 'We can't get out. The walls are smooth as glass and there aren't any trees, and the gate's locked.'

Mary looked round her. He was right. Doctor Dee's house stood in a square garden which was surrounded by a very high wall. There was not a tree, not a creeper, nothing by which the walls could be climbed. And even in the starlight she could see the enormous padlock on the gate. 'But – how did you get in, then?'

'Walked in,' said Peter bitterly. 'I thought I heard Gib mewing inside the walls, so of course I came straight in. And the gate shut behind me, smooth as butter, and I've been here for hours. Mother and Daddy will be out of their minds. They've probably got the police out looking for me by now. It must be midnight.'

'Probably after,' said Mary, for whom the night had certainly seemed a long one. 'Well, we'll have to fly out the way I came in. Hold tight to Gib, will you?'

'Then it's true? It *is* magic?'

'It was magic that locked the gate on you,' said Mary, 'you can be sure of that. But I've got some too, I told you. There's a snag about this broomstick – it's Doctor Dee's, and I may not be able to make it take us home, but at least it'll get us over the wall.' She felt for the remains of the fly-by-night in her pocket, and squeezed the last of its juices over her hand. 'Hurry up now, hold tight. These broomsticks are funny, they sometimes buck.'

But it didn't buck. When Mary rubbed it with the fly-by-night, with a sharp command to 'get over the wall, and then fly to Red Manor – Red Manor, in Shropshire. Do you hear?' the broomstick tried its best, rearing from the ground, but with the double weight on it, it could not rise even as far as the top of the wall. At about six feet up, it stuck, and then careered round and round the walled garden till the two children were dizzy, and Mary gasped at last, 'Go down, will you? *Go down!*'

With a little wriggle of relief, the broomstick dropped. The two children got off. There was no need to hold on to the cats now; Tib and Gib seemed to realise exactly what the situation was, and were silent, each cat clinging tightly to a child's shoulder with every one of his eighteen claws.

'What on earth are we going to do?' asked Peter in dismay. Then suddenly he lifted his head. 'Listen! What's that?'

Above the soughing of the wind in the treetops outside came another sound; a high, swishing noise that Mary, with a prickling of the spine, recognised.

'It's a broomstick coming. Doctor Dee. Quickly, we'll have to hide!'

'He'll find us in two minutes. There's only those bushes, no other cover at all in the garden, and the house door's locked. I tried it. I wanted to see if there was a telephone – this is a fine time to giggle, I must say! Girls!' He seized her arm. 'Get into the bushes, quickly. It's the only chance!'

But Mary ran for the house door. 'No. I told you I had magic. I can open locks.' And she dragged torch and book from her pocket, flashing the light at the pages.

Peter was quick. He saw the point straight away – even though, thought Mary admiringly, he had hardly had time to get used to the idea of magic at all. 'Can you? Then if you open the house door, he'll think we've got in somehow, and we can get out through the garden gate while he's busy searching the house. Is that it?'

'We may not even need to open the garden gate.' In Mary's hand, the torch had found the right page, and fixed on the lock-spell. 'He's bringing another broomstick. We'll have one each. Wait, now.' She muttered the lock-spell straight to the house door, and watched it open immediately to stand wide on a dark hall. There was a gasp behind her, but when she turned Peter and the grey cat had disappeared. She ran across the grass, snatched up the broomstick, and ran with Tib in among the bushes, to crouch down beside Peter.

Not a moment too soon. Low overhead came that long swishing noise, like paper tearing, and a broomstick bearing a black crouching figure shot over the top of the garden wall and landed on the grass with a thud.

Doctor Dee was furiously angry. The screech he gave when he saw the open door made Mary shrink back into the bushes, and she felt Peter shiver beside her. There was a soft hiss from the grey cat, but it did not move. Tib made no sound. Doctor Dee jumped off his broomstick, flung it angrily to one side, and rushed in through the open door of the house, his white wand of power brandished above his head.

'So I've caught you, young witch!' they heard him shouting. 'Destroy my laboratory too, would you? We shall see! Gormbridge or no Gormbridge, professor or no professor, we shall see!'

He was searching the house. From window after window, as he searched, they saw the flickering green light from his wand.

The children watched it. It appeared, suddenly, at an upstairs window. Then it faded.

Peter said softly, 'He's at the back of the house now. Come on.'

They ran out on to the lawn, and Mary picked up the broomstick the doctor had flung aside. She could feel it quivering with apprehension – or could it be rage?

'It's my own little broomstick!' she whispered, excited and relieved. 'And it knows the way home! Here, you take Doctor Dee's. If it will only follow mine —'

But it would not. As Peter took it, it gave a jump and a buck, and tore itself free from his hands. It vanished after its master into the dark doorway of the house.

'It'll go straight to him!' exclaimed Peter in dismay. 'He'll know for certain you're here! Quick, Mary, get on your own broomstick and go now. He doesn't even know I'm here – I'll be all right. And in the morning —'

But Mary was already running for the gate. 'We'll go together, or not at all. We've got magic, we'll manage somehow. For tonight I'm a witch, just as he says.'

And indeed, it seemed that she was. She had, in her haste, let go the little broomstick, but it came cantering alongside her. She did not even need the torch and the book for the lock-spell. She whipped the last fragment of fly-by-night from the pocket of her coat, and, pressing it hard against the padlock, whispered the spell as quickly as she could gabble the words.

The padlock snapped with a flash of green fire, and fell to the ground. The door opened on screaming hinges that sounded like a screech of rage. They heard its echo, in Doctor Dee's voice, from the house behind them. Then they tumbled through the open gate into the starlight of a narrow, winding lane.

'Get on!' cried Mary, and in a moment Peter was behind her on the broomstick, the grey cat clamped to his shoulder and hissing now with excitement like a steam kettle. Tib was still silent, but every now and again his tail whipped from side to side, as if he could not stop it. 'Hang on, everyone!' she shouted. 'Now, dear little broomstick, please take us all home to Red Manor!'

And she rubbed her fly-by-night hand down the shaft of the broom.

You could feel that it was an effort, but the little broomstick tried very gallantly. It heaved itself into the air under the double weight of children and cats, and surged up three feet, four feet, five . . .

At about eight feet it levelled off, and began to race.

The tops of the high lane hedges were just level with their knees. Now and again the branches of trees loomed up in the dark and whipped at them. They lay as low as they could, holding on tightly.

It seemed this was as high as they could get, and at this height the sensation of speed was infinitely greater than it had been through the limitless air or over the wide seas of cloud. Both children were soon breathless, and Mary heard Tib begin to swear to himself as he clung, rocking, to her shoulder. The lane was full of curves, and the broomstick went swooping round them, banking to right and left like a swallow flying. It was terrifying, exhilarating, and very uncomfortable. But they were on the way home, and, providing they met no obstacle more than eight or nine feet high, they stood a good chance of getting there.

Then they heard the other broomstick coming. It was high overhead, with Doctor Dee, still shouting angrily, astride it. And it was overhauling them rapidly. Mary waited for his yell of recognition as he sighted them below him. But instead his voice changed to a shout of greeting as another long, tearing swish announced the arrival of a new broomstick, and Madam Mumble-chook's voice, high-pitched and furious, cried, 'Have you caught her?'

Craning her neck, Mary could just see the two of them high above, shadows flying against the windy stars. Green sparks streamed from the wand of power. It lit the figures of Madam and Doctor Dee, crouched low on their racing broomsticks, peering around, peering . . .

Any minute now, thought Mary, they would be seen. At the same moment the little broomstick, as if it read her thought, dropped smoothly downwards until it was running in the lane's shadow.

It was very dark here, and the broomstick's pace, mercifully, slowed. They were free now of the whipping branches, but still the curves and dips of the lane, which the little broomstick seemed to sense as accurately as a night-flying bat, continually took them by surprise, so that they lurched and swayed more violently than ever, and had to hang on with all their strength. It was like riding an uncontrollable horse at full gallop in the dark along a path one doesn't know.

And with much faster horses behind one. The other broomsticks were almost level now, high overhead.

'Remember they don't know I'm here,' whispered Peter. 'They think it's only you with the two cats. They'll expect you to be away ahead of them at full speed. If we stop here in the lane and wait, they'll overfly us, and get out of sight ahead. Then we can go home our own way.'

Mary opened her mouth to say the word, but at that very moment the lane came to an end, and the little broomstick shot out of the comforting shadow of the hedgerows, across a smooth open meadow where, sharp below them on the starlit grass, scudded their flying shadow.

CHAPTER XII

Ride away, ride away,
Peter shall ride,
He shall have a pussy cat
Tied to one side

TOO late to go back. Too late even to make for the shadow of one of the huge oaks dotted here and there in the meadow. They had been seen. From high above came the twin screams of anger and discovery.

'There she goes!' shrieked Madam Mumblechook, and the Doctor shouted at the same time:

'Two of them! She had an accomplice all the time! Look, two of them on the same broomstick!'

'And that,' cried Madam, 'means they can't go any higher! Sitting ducks, dear Doctor, sitting ducks! We've got them both! Are you ready? You take the port, I'll take the starboard! Now – *attack*!'

The two broomsticks, high in the night air, wheeled away from one another, then tilted, turned, and dived. Their speed was tremendous. They tore downwards on a steadily rising scream of air, one from each side, deadly as hawks plummeting on their prey.

Mary felt the little broomstick give a sudden leap of

effort, and thought, without hope, that it was trying its best to accelerate. But no. It dropped another two feet, so that the children's toes were brushing the dew from the long, seeding grasses. Harebells shook with a sweet, whispering rattle. Tansies swept their legs with dew. A thistle exploded softly against Mary's foot, its cloud of seeds scattering like ghosts through the dim grass.

She gripped the broomstick more tightly. 'Please – please! Oh, Peter, it's going to land and let them —'

'No,' said Peter urgently, in her ear. 'Leave it alone. It knows what it's about. Don't you see? They can't pounce on us when we're flying as low as this. Coming down from that height they'd run straight into the ground, and bash themselves and their broomsticks to bits. Unless they can actually force us to land, they can't do a thing . . .'

His voice was lost in the whining scream as Doctor Dee swept down on them. The little broomstick had held steadily to its course, sailing forward straight and level, but in the exact moment that the Doctor swooped, it jinked sideways, so that the clinging children lurched with it and their right feet struck the ground. Their steed checked for a moment, but recovered immediately and leaped away. The attacking broomstick overshot them at great speed. For a moment it looked as if the Doctor would hit the ground, but at the last instant he recovered, and his broomstick tore on, away, rearing upwards fast to regain height.

'Feet up,' gasped Peter. 'Lie as flat as you can!'

As Mary obeyed him, the other broomstick came down to the attack. Madam was bolder than the Doctor, or else her broom was not so well under control. She came down at terrific speed, so fast that her yell of triumph was torn half away by the wind of the dive.

'The familiars! The familiars as well! We have them all! Now land, you little fools, land, or you will be hurt!'

She was on them. Her grabbing hand brushed Mary's hair. The little broomstick stopped dead, sat back on its bristles for one bone-rattling moment, then switched clear round like a horse turning on its haunches, and sped away at right angles over the meadow.

Madam Mumblechook had been travelling too fast to stop or turn. Mary, looking back, saw her hit the ground. At the last moment her broomstick shied, met the ground in a long, tearing skid, then, rearing sharply, shot straight up into the air again. In front of it, suddenly, loomed the black bulk of a tree. The broomstick swerved, but fractionally too late. It struck the outer branches of the tree, lurched, side-slipped, and threw its rider. Madam Mumblechook, her grip loosened by the near-crash, hurtled off in a tangle of flying black skirts, to hang like a ragged old crow, screeching, in the high boughs of the tree.

'That'll teach her!' said Peter with satisfaction. 'I told you our broomstick knew what it was doing. Look, I think it's saved us!'

On the words the little broomstick, rising slightly in a flowing leap, crossed a fence and a wide ditch that smelled of meadowsweet, and ran with them into the shadow of a deep, dark wood.

Just before the trees closed round them they heard Madam cry, 'Doctor Dee! Doctor Dee!' There was an answering shout from high above, then the whistling track of his broomstick curved away and back towards the top of the oak.

'That should keep them busy!' said Peter cheerfully.

Mary was patting the little broomstick with her fly-by-night hand. This seemed to give it pleasure; it gave little jumps and curvets as it carried them swiftly along a curly path through the trees. The going here was more difficult even than it had been in the lane, for the path was narrow, and the wood, consisting of big trees set widely apart, was thick with undergrowth. Trails of ivy and honeysuckle hung from the boughs; holly and elder and hazel clustered thickly between the huge trunks of oak and beech; there were ferns everywhere, and the seeding heads of foxgloves rattled as their feet struck them in passing. In the darkness it was like a jungle.

'This must lead us home in the end,' said Mary, voicing the thought for both of them. 'The little broomstick must know the way. The only thing is, it'll take an awfully long time. It seemed ages, even flying.' As quickly as she could, she told him of her adventure. 'How long did it take you, Peter, without a broomstick? And how *did* you get here, anyway?'

'I had my bike for part of the way. Somebody told me they thought they'd seen Gib down in the garden of an empty house near the river – I don't know if you know it? Well, I went that way, but there was thick mist at the river bridge, so I left my bike there, and walked. It was easier. I thought I heard Gib, you see, calling in the mist. I suppose that may have been magic, too? Anyway, I lost my way in the mist, and couldn't get back, and then I found Doctor Dee's house.'

'How far from the bridge?' asked Mary.

'I don't know. I seemed to be walking for ages, but – hallo, I can see the end of the wood. That's a pity; I hoped it would take us the whole way. If they're waiting for us at the other side —'

'They're probably still stuck at the tree,' said Mary hopefully, 'or her broomstick's run away, or —'

She stopped. Unmistakably, just above the crests of the woodland trees, they could hear Madam Mumblechook and the Doctor, talking. The two of them must be flying a short way apart; their voices were raised, and quite distinct.

'. . . in the wood. I saw it distinctly. We have only to wait up here, cruising,' said Doctor Dee clearly, 'to see which way they break cover. Then we have them.'

'Has it occurred to you, my dear Doctor —' Madam had, it appeared, quite recovered from her mishap— 'has it occurred to you that the girl must have the Master Spell? How else could she have undone all those expert transformations, and destroyed our laboratory and all our years of work, all in a moment? Everything went, everything; all the main building. It was impossible to get the fire under control until it reached the boarders' wing – then it went straight out of its own accord. Certainly caused by the Master Spell. It must have been perfectly true that her name was Smith. When we catch her, dear Doctor, it will need care, but I feel sure that we can deal with her —'

Here for a moment, mercifully, the conversation was lost in a gust of wind that combed the treetops. But when this ceased the voices were nearer, right overhead. They seemed to be circling.

'. . . offer you the hospitality of my house,' Doctor Dee was saying. 'My resources, compared with those of the College, are small indeed, but I venture to think, dear Madam, that you will find my own small laboratory very well equipped, very well equipped indeed. More than adequate,' he added with a nasty chuckle, 'to deal even with Miss Mary Smith, Gormbridge or no.'

'But the Master Spell,' said Madam Mumblechook anxiously, 'the Master Spell?'

'Only works till daylight, even for a genuine Mary Smith,' said Doctor Dee with another chuckle. 'All we have to do is to keep them contained in this wood till daylight, then run them down at leisure. Unless of course they decide to stay there and hide, in which case —'

'We simply starve them out,' said Madam Mumblechook with satisfaction.

'Exactly,' said Doctor Dee. 'And now, dear lady, if we gain a little height we shall be able to watch all sides of this wood at once.'

His voice dwindled as the two broomsticks rose. The sound of their circling grew fainter, but was still there, a background to the swishing progress of the children's own steed through the ferns.

The children did not speak. It was too bad. All they could do was to leave it to the little broomstick. But it seemed as if the little broomstick had understood. All of a sudden, a few yards short of the starlit gap that showed the end of the wood, it stopped and sank back on its twigs. Peter got off without a word, and walked forward to the fence.

Then he came back. 'It's another open field, a big one, sloping down to what looks like a stream. A few trees there, but not enough – not thick cover like this. And beyond that it looks just like open moor.'

'What are we going to do?'

Peter patted the little broomstick, absently. He cleared his throat. 'Look, this is silly. I heard what they said. It's obvious what we ought to do. I told you before, in Doctor Dee's garden. If I stay here and you go on, then at least one of us stands a good chance. You take both cats, and we could arrange a signal. If I broke out of the opposite side of the wood and drew them off, that would give you a start. And if there was only you on the broomstick it could get you well above cloud before they realised what had happened. And with that start—'

'But what about you?'

'Oh, I'd be all right. I'd dodge back in before they saw it was only me.'

'But,' said Mary, 'it's not like it was in Doctor Dee's garden. They know you're in here. Once they realised you hadn't even got a broomstick – and they'd guess what had happened, sooner or later – they'd come in and look for you.'

'They'd never find me. It's dark.'

'And in the morning?'

'Well,' said Peter, 'it's a big wood. I'd climb a tree or something. And you'd be on your way back, by then, with help.'

'On a broomstick?' asked Mary. 'With the Vicar – your father – and Constable Buffin and old Zebedee following on bicycles?'

In spite of their plight, Peter laughed. 'Well, I suppose you couldn't use the broomstick.'

'I don't know the way without the broomstick,' said

Mary grimly. 'And you say you don't, either. It's no good, Peter. We'll have to get out of this together, or not at all.'

She hesitated, pulling a frond of fern absently between her fingers. Then she looked straight at him. (It was strange to remember that shy and stiff Mary Smith of two days ago, who could never have spoken like this.) 'And don't think I haven't realised that you've tried to save me twice, Peter, and risked yourself to do it. But it's together, or nothing.'

'O.K.,' said Peter easily. He, thought Mary, must never have been shy in his life. 'Well, we have to think of something else. What about this Master Spell? Isn't there something in the book that'll help?'

'No. I've been thinking, and there isn't. There's only the Master Spell itself, and that simply undoes any magic that's in reach. It would un-magick our own little broomstick, too. And even if I went, and left you the Master Spell to protect you, you might never find your way home again, or we mightn't be able to find you.' She turned her head to look at the gap of starlight at the end of the path. 'I have a feeling that we're in a very different country from our own, and it isn't just distance that separates them.'

'Look,' said Peter, 'don't sound so worried! We've done all right so far, haven't we? We'll think of something. In any case, I'd be nervous of using that Master Spell of yours. Just think if I did it when your broomstick was still in range, and getting you nicely up to five hundred feet or so! Well, let's think what to do.'

'Give the little broomstick a rest, first,' said Mary, 'and maybe groom it a bit. It seems to like that.' And she dismounted and stood stroking it with her fly-by-night hand.

It certainly seemed to like that. It rubbed itself against her, purring . . .

No, of course it wasn't purring. Mary turned her head, sharply. It was Tib, beside her ear, who had suddenly purred. And his head was up and his ears cocked towards where, deep in the wood, someone – something – was approaching them.

CHAPTER XIII

The birds are singing, the bells are ringing,
The wild deer come galloping by, by

'SOMEONE'S coming,' said Peter sharply. 'Get on quick. It sounds as if one of them's beating the wood to flush us out, while the other —'

'No,' said Mary. 'Tib's purring. And look, the little broomstick hasn't moved. Keep still and listen.'

They waited, quite still, their eyes on the darkness of the deep wood. The rustling grew louder. It was not one person, but a crowd of people or creatures approaching softly through the thick undergrowth. Ferns swished and the dew shook down. All the scents of the wood came floating, larch and bramble-flowers and late honeysuckle, and the dark smoky scent of ivy. Then the bushes parted, and into the dim starlight, the dew shining on antlers and burnished coat, stepped a big, beautiful stag. After him, delicately, trooped a score of dappled deer.

Tib gave a queer, gobbling cry, deep in his throat, the cry Mary had last heard in the dreadful strong-room. On Peter's shoulder, the grey cat mewed softly, and began to purr.

'It's the deer that were enchanted!' said Mary excitedly. 'I freed them with the Master Spell. Perhaps they've come to help us!'

The stag paced forward, stretching his splendid head towards her. He snuffed twice, at her, at Tib on her shoulder, then turned to look at Peter, ears pricked.

'Peter's my friend,' said Mary quickly. 'He came to rescue Gib.'

The great stag reached forward to snuff at Peter's chest, then he wheeled, trotted forward to the fence that edged the wood and stood there, his magnificent head high, looking back at them over his shoulder.

'I remember him,' said Mary. 'He was that poor creature covered with mangy fur. Madam laughed at him and prodded him. I'm sure he's come to help us. But how? What can he do?'

'He wants us to go that way,' said Peter. 'Come along.'

But Mary hung back. 'I don't see how we can. Listen, you can still hear those two overhead.'

The other deer were all around them now, crowding close. Peter laughed, pointing to the tossing heads and bright liquid eyes. 'It's a convoy.' He sounded quite cheerful and confident. 'Don't you see? If we break out of the wood in the middle of that lot, Madam and the Doctor certainly can't get at us – even if they see us. And they might miss us completely among all the running shadows. Come along. It's our best chance.'

'Do you really think —' began Mary doubtfully, but

was stopped by the little broomstick. It could hardly be said to be tossing its head and pawing the ground, but the effect was the same. It pranced in her hands, obviously excited, and willing them to go. 'All right!' she said, and jumped on. 'Hang on then, Tib! Jump for it, Peter, or the little broomstick'll be away with me!'

Peter jumped astride the broomstick, and held on. The cats clung tightly, both purring now like racing engines. Round them the deer leaped and frolicked, their delicate hoofs hardly printing the ground, and with them the little broomstick skipped, frisking. The great stag threw his head up, snuffed the air, then, from a standstill, leaped the fence and trotted out into the starlight. After him streamed the deer, and among them, a shadow among their leaping shadows, ran the little broomstick.

Smoothly over the fence, over the ditch, out into the open field – then all at once they were galloping, the deer travelling in long, fluid leaps all around them. Antlers tossed, eyes shone wide and dark in the starlight, white tails scudded ahead, dainty hoofs pattered on turf like rain. The dew-laden coats brushed the children's legs, and under them the grassy meadow flashed by as, effortless, the herd raced as silently as their own shadows down the long slope towards the stream. A hedge showed, briefly, and was gone under them as if it had been no more than a stand of thistles. The stream, shining and noisy, flashed under them and fled back into silence. A stone wall loomed, and the little broomstick, gathering itself, flung itself and its load up and over as the deer soared and sank like a great wave breaking, and the race went on.

Then suddenly the birds were with them, too. A

peewit tumbled screaming out of the dark, then a flight of swallows, with a high shrilling noise, then blackbirds, thrushes, pigeons, sparrows – all the birds fresh from those dreadful cages; birds who should have been asleep, head under wing, but who flew now with the herd of deer to hide the escaping children from the danger above them.

For the danger was there. For the first few minutes, it seemed, Madam and the Doctor had assumed that the stream of shadows breaking at a gallop from the wood was only a wild herd of deer; but they must have decided to make sure, for now one broomstick turned quickly in pursuit. The other still circled sentinel above the trap of trees.

It was Doctor Dee who was coming. There was the dreadful, familiar swish of his broomstick overhead. Then the sudden fierce swoop, which scattered the birds in all directions, and the yell of anger and triumph: 'Madam! Madam! Here! This way!'

Then with the white wand brandished in his hand like a whip, Doctor Dee was swooping down among the birds, scattering them to right and left as he tried to reach the children in the middle of the racing herd.

But the herd defeated him. Each time the wand whipped down it struck some tossing antler, and the green sparks flew and flashed, but still the deer fled on unharmed. They were not afraid; he could not enchant them again; they only bunched more closely round the children, and raced on. The wizard whipped at them with the powerless wand, and the green fire ran along their coats like water. Mary saw, then, that all the animals nearest to them were the stags, all armed with antlers. Once, when the wand flashed down near her head, a pair

of antlers caught and parried it with a crack and blaze
like lightning, and the wizard gave a cry as if he had had
a shock. After that he withdrew to a height of perhaps
twenty feet, and once again the birds closed in.

But not just defending now; this time they attacked.
And they, too, were immune to the strokes of the white
wand. They were all too small to damage Doctor Dee
himself – the biggest were the pigeons – but it is not easy
to fly straight through a flock of wheeling, darting,
furious birds, who think nothing of flying straight into
one's face, or hitting out with passing claws at one's head,
or simply blinding one by flying round and round in
flocks at the level of one's eyes. And the Doctor's broomstick didn't like it, either. It swerved and bucked and
tried to jib, while the Doctor, hanging on with one hand
and swiping blindly round him with the wand in the
other, came once or twice very near to falling off.

But not quite. And, as mile after swift mile went by,
Mary and Peter could see that the deer were beginning
to tire. And above Doctor Dee, still fresh, and too clever
to come down into the swirl of birds and defending
antlers, sailed Madam Mumblechook.

They were on a slope now, a long slope running
downhill. Here and there were tufts of rushes; they
brushed the bellies of the running deer and swished past
the children's feet. Beside them now, on the right, was
the bright rush and noise of water. A river. A swift river,
rushing down through stony rapids and over steep, white
falls. Then suddenly, about a quarter of a mile away, at
the foot of the long slope, they saw what seemed to be a
wide stretch of water.

The sea? thought Mary, and for the first time felt

despair. If they had to cross a sea, without the deer, with perhaps only the frail help of the birds . . . and if the little broomstick tired . . .

'It's the mist!' cried Peter. 'I told you I got lost in it on the way here. If we get through that, we'll know the way home!'

On down the slope, with the drumming of the tiny hoofs all round them. Now she could see.

It was indeed the mist, a great, white lake of mist, thick and rolling like cloud. The starlight was bright on the surface of it. The river rushed and cascaded right into it and was lost, as if there really was a sea or a lake below. But at least, once in the shelter of that thick cloud, they would need no escort, no cover. They could run at the broomstick's own pace, safe and shrouded, till perhaps on the other side they would see the familiar yellow lights of home.

The cloud of birds was already wheeling, ghostly, in and out of the edges of the mist. The herd went down the last slope with a slither and scatter of turf, then slowed, trotted, stopped on the long stony strand where the river met the mist.

The big stag turned, the vapour swirling round his shoulders like cloud. The herd parted to let the children through into the safe shelter of the mist.

Then with a yell and a last, desperate swoop, Doctor Dee dived on them like a stone falling.

He almost reached them. But the great stag leaped clear into the air, straight over their heads, and his antlers struck the wizard's wand clean out of his hand. The wand flew wide. It struck the surface of the river. There was a hiss like steam as the green fire ran to and fro across the water, then a flash, a crack, a spurt of white smoke, and the wand vanished into the swirling river.

Behind the children was another crack, a flurry, then a crash. Past Mary's cheek went the broken half of a broom-handle, and a scatter of birch-twigs. Then everything dimmed and vanished; stag, deer, birds, starlight all blotted out as their own little broomstick, undamaged, plunged forward with them into the cloud of mist.

CHAPTER XIV
Home again, home again,
Journey's done

THE mist was not so very thick after all. Once, momentarily, they ran through a thinning patch of it which showed a glimpse of sky, and Peter spoke breathlessly in Mary's ear.

'She's still there. High up. I don't think she saw us.'

'She can't attack us here. I think it's water underneath,' said Mary. 'As long as we stay low enough, we're safe.'

'And when we come out of it we'll be on our own side, I'm sure of that. But how do we know she can't follow us there? After all, we've been on *her* side of the mist.'

Mary was silent for a moment. This was something she had not thought of. But it was reasonable, after all. If the magic fly-by-night had worked at Red Manor, then it was possible that they would not be safe from Madam Mumblechook even on their own side of the mist.

She tried to keep the nervousness out of her voice. 'But

she can't take the cats back, and would she follow us just to get revenge?'

'I expect she wants her Master Spell book back,' said Peter.

'Oh! Of course she does . . . Then we'll have to use it somehow, won't we, to protect ourselves. But how? Let's think . . .'

'Let's not take the trouble,' said Peter. He sounded light-hearted. 'As soon as we're near home, you can chant your spell, and chant it as loud as you please. It'll bring her broomstick down sharpish, and once we're in our own fields, it won't matter if it un-magicks ours as well.'

'But our dear little broomstick —'

'*Wants* to be un-magicked,' said Peter. 'Can't you feel it?'

And indeed, the broomstick had given a little skip and a bound or two, and quickened its already headlong pace through the mist.

'Don't you see?' asked Peter. 'It's probably enchanted, too, and it's tired of having to rush about at all hours, and wait where it's told, and carry tiresome old witches around all the time —'

'Thank you very much,' said Mary.

'Well, I didn't mean you. Anyway, I'm sure it's as much prison for the broomsticks as it was for the birds and deer. That's why they behave so badly. If they *liked* it, would they buck and try to throw people, like naughty ponies?'

'I think you're right,' said Mary. 'It only obeyed me because of the fly-by-night.'

'What was that?'

'A kind of spell, I suppose.' She told him about it, quickly.

'Well, there you are,' said Peter. 'And I think it's helping us now because we were kind to it. But it'll just love to be rid of the spell, and go off free on its own, and kick up its heels when it feels like it. Won't you, little bizzom?'

And Mary, feeling the little broomstick wriggle and jump in reply, thought Peter was probably right. In any case, they had to get rid of Madam Mumblechook somehow, and the only way to do it was by using the Master Spell. But they would have to time it correctly, or it could mean disaster for them all . . .

She was opening her mouth to say so, when Peter's hand touched her arm, and she realised that the mist was thinning round them. There was darkness ahead that looked solid, and from time to time a glimpse of darkness below that did not seem so solid, but that caught and reflected stray gleams like water rippling.

And daylight was coming. Around them the faint light touched the mist, hazing it with colour. In a short time, the Master Spell would be powerless.

Then all at once they ran out from the covering mist, over a narrow strand where pebbles gleamed and the faint waves crisped and whispered. Then up over a meadowland starred with daisies showing pale already in the growing light.

As they ran clear of the mist they heard Madam Mumblechook's voice behind them, high above.

'Stop!' cried Mary, and the little broomstick stopped and sat down. The children, slipping from its back, looked up the way they had come.

She was there, some way back, high over the lake of mist. She must have been cruising to and fro above them, waiting, as she and Doctor Dee had waited above the wood, to see where they would break cover. Behind her the sky was growing pale, the stars fading already into a strip of swimming and luminous rose. But the magic round her still shone green and baleful, and the sparks spurted from under her broomstick as she hauled it round sharply in mid-air and set it on a course straight for the little group on the ground.

'I have you!' she shrilled. 'I have you now! My book! My book!' And she put her broomstick into a dive.

The cats were hissing; even Peter was looking scared. Mary whipped the book out of her pocket, and groped for the torch. But she did not need it. The book fell open in her hands at the Master Spell, and there on the page the words glowed clear and red. Standing straight and without moving a step, while the light grew and the dawn came and the witch tore down towards them like a baleful star, Mary began, loudly and very clearly, to recite the Master Spell.

The witch heard it. They saw her urge her broomstick faster, faster, to force it down to earth before the spell came to an end. They saw her glance over her shoulder at the growing light, which would take from Mary the power the spell gave her. But it was no use. Madam Mumblechook was still well up above the mist, and the last of the stars were still visible, when, triumphantly, Mary finished.

'. . . the dancing ring of days!' called Mary (or something like it), and, as before, several things happened at once.

The flying broomstick lost way and plunged, as suddenly as a falling stone, into the mist. There was a yell, an enormous splash, then silence except for a hiss like metal cooling, and a sudden agitated lapping of water on the pebbled shore. Beside the children, the little broomstick gave a leap, a buck, a funny little flick of its birch-twigs, and vanished. And with a splash of gold and red and lovely light, the sun came up.

The two children, with the two cats, looked about them as the golden light grew.

They were standing in a long meadow where cows grazed, apparently unalarmed by what had happened. In front of them was a narrow strip of shingle which edged, not a lake of mist, but a river. The mist had gone. And the river was vaguely familiar to Mary.

'There,' said Peter suddenly, 'by the bridge. That's my bicycle. I thought I knew the place. It's only three miles home from here. Can you hang on behind?'

She hadn't even been missed. The front door at Red Manor was still unlocked, and after the children had said goodbye – 'And see you in the morning,' said Peter – Mary let herself and Tib in quietly, locked the door behind her, and crept up to her bedroom. The grandfather clock, coming up to five o'clock, merely winked its brass at her and ticked calmly on.

Her room was as she had left it, with one difference. The fly-by-night had vanished from her tooth-glass. And when she took off her coat and put a hand in the pocket, she found only a torch. The book of Master Spells had vanished, too.

And padding round in circles on the quilt, purring,

looking very contented and very sleepy indeed – as well he might – was a very ordinary cat, who would never, Mary knew, try to be a witch's cat again.

'I have had a letter from your parents,' said Great-Aunt Charlotte later that morning.

She had come down, early for her, while Mary was still finishing breakfast. For a moment Mary felt alarmed, thinking that her great-aunt must know something about the night's adventures, but Great-Aunt Charlotte was as placid as usual, and obviously pleased with the news she bore.

'They are coming back at the beginning of October,' said Great-Aunt Charlotte, 'and I am delighted to say that they talk of buying a house in this part of the country. There is a delightful house about three miles from here, which will be vacant soon. It has an excellent garden, which includes a stretch of the river. What is it, child?'

'Is it near a bridge?' asked Mary.

'Bridge? Of course they play bridge. That is one of the reasons why it will be so delightful to have them near us. Your mother tends to be a little erratic, but your father plays an excellent game, and the dear Vicar —'

'I meant – well, it doesn't matter,' said Mary. 'I know the house, Aunt Charlotte. It's very nice. And it'll be lovely living near here.'

'And not so lonely for you, with your brother and sister here?' Great-Aunt Charlotte patted her shoulder, kindly. 'But I have more good news for you. The Vicar – our own Vicar – came home yesterday. His son Peter is a boy

about your own age. It will be pleasant for both of you to
have a companion, I am sure.'

'That will be lovely.' Mary had kept her eyes on her
plate while her great-aunt spoke. Now she looked up.
'Aunt Charlotte, if we come to live here, could I keep
Tib, please?'

'Tib? Oh, the cat. I see no reason why not, if your
parents make no objection. And Confucius certainly does
not care for him. In fact, I am not at all sure if he even
belongs to the house? Do you know, Miss Marshbanks?'

'He does not belong here,' said Miss Marjoribanks with
decision. 'And he certainly seems to have strangely taken
to Mary.'

Mary looked down at her plate again. Miss Marjoribanks had – it seemed to her – been watching her very
narrowly indeed this morning. Was it possible that she
had heard something? Or even seen?

'Well,' said Great-Aunt Charlotte placidly, 'Mrs
McLeod will know. We can ask her. Now, dear child,
enjoy yourself. I think I shall go and see Zebedee about
the roses.'

She dropped an absent kiss on Mary's cheek, and
went out, with Confucius waddling behind her. Miss
Marjoribanks rose, rang for Mrs McLeod to clear, and
went briskly to her chair to get her knitting. It was,
thought Mary, going to be the usual busy day, except
that now she was going to see Peter, and Tib was going
with her.

At that exact moment – perhaps a little of the magic
still clung about him – Tib jumped on to the window-sill
outside. Mary went across to open the window. It was a
brilliantly sunny day, and Zebedee was on the lawn

sweeping up the leaves with his big broomstick, a normal, ordinary broomstick that did exactly as he told it.

The click of knitting needles suddenly stopped. Looking up, Mary caught Miss Marjoribanks watching the broomstick, too, still with that strange look in her eyes.

Suddenly, memories came back to her; the rushing and crackling of twigs on that first night when Tib leaped to her window-sill – the crash of a heavy body hurtling down too fast on an unmanageable broomstick. Then there was Miss Marjoribanks' stiffness at breakfast next morning, and the way she and Tib had looked at one another. Finally, there was the memory of someone, somewhere – this memory was vague and misty, and getting all the time vaguer – of someone writing in an enormous book, for the second time: '*Mary Smith, Red Manor, Shropſhire . . .*'

Mary saw it now. Poor Miss Marjoribanks had been Tib's first choice, but she hadn't liked Tib, so she had never found the fly-by-night, never had the power to manage the little broomstick, open the locks, find – what was it she had found, and where?

Beside her Tib purred, arching himself against her. She stooped to whisper in his ear:

'You tried us both, didn't you, to get your friend Gib back from . . . from wherever it was. Poor Miss Marshbanks! She'll never know what she missed – that adventure . . .'

She paused. Later, when she had caught up on her sleep, no doubt she would remember it all perfectly . . .

Miss Marjoribanks, who would never know what she had missed, was unwrapping a new hank of wool in a rather nasty green shade.

'It is delightful, my dear, that your parents should be thinking of moving near us. Of course it will mean that you will have to board at school, but no doubt you will enjoy that? Of course you will – and indeed needs must, since —' She paused, and fixed Mary with her eye — 'since there is no school near here of any kind.' She paused again. 'Of any kind,' she repeated, firmly.

'Not now, anyway,' said Mary softly, to Tib, who was sitting beside her.

Tib smirked.

Nobody ever quite knew how the birch-grove came to be there, down beside the river, just near the old stone bridge. They grew like magic, those birches – or so said Mary's father, who had bought the field along with the nearby house. And very soon there they were, full-grown, golden in spring and green in summer, and in autumn rich with orange and russet and amber and all the colours of sunset.

But in winter, when the trees were bare, the colour of dark raisins, bloomy with purple against the high windy sky, you could hear the wind swishing through them, whistling like something flying; and the myriad tiny twigs rattled like the hoofs of galloping deer, and overhead the birds tumbled, crying and shrilling, in the winter sky.

But Mary, who was away at school, and seldom went down to the woods in winter, never heard it.

And if she had, she would not have remembered.

Author's Note

IT is possible that some readers may not believe in magic broomsticks. I can only quote the letter I received from Messrs Harrods, Ltd, in reply to my queries about prices of the available range.

'Obviously the demand for this product is limited and, with modern ideas regarding colour, weight, and the use of plastics, quite apart from a desire for comfort, they can only be made to a very special order. During the past few years the HELIBROOM has been found increasingly popular both as a means of transport and, when use is made of the remote control system available at extra charge, for the traditional clearing-up-the-garden-rubbish. May we suggest one made from carbon-fibre reinforced plastic with nylon bristles. This could be obtained in black, brown, or in pastel shades. The two-stroke engine is made of aluminium to save weight, and so are the rotors. Greasing is only needed every 100 years or 1,000,000 miles. Accessories which can be supplied at extra cost are a matching telescope and a coffee percolator.

The work is specialised, and there may be a delay of several years in obtaining the HELIBROOM, so we would appreciate prompt confirmation of any order. The basic cost would be £874.75.'

I believe there is now a cheaper German model available, but the report in last month's *Whoosh* was unfavourable. The Helibroom remains the best buy.

M.S.